S0-DZC-303

*Ruth doesn't like having demands put on her friendships.*

"Well, the way you are rushing to his defense obviously betrays your feelings, Ruth. I'm shocked that you would take up with someone you know so little about. A miner, as compared to a man like Dr. Bradley."

"Mrs. Greenwood, I am not 'taking up,' as you put it, with anyone who is disreputable. Even so, I think I am the one to judge my friends, rather than you and Mr. Greenwood. I know you mean well, but I have begun to feel pressured to encourage Dr. Bradley's attention. I won't do that. While I respect his profession, I have no interest in him as a suitor. So maybe we can put that matter to rest, once and for all."

Mrs. Greenwood turned for the door. "In that case, I'll be leaving. You obviously resent my concern. I was mistaken to think you appreciated the fact that we cared about you, but I see that I have misjudged you. You are far too headstrong for your own good, young lady." Flinging that parting shot over her shoulder, she stormed out, slamming the door behind her.

Ruth glared at the door, seething with anger. She fought an urge to yank the door open and tell her if she cared about her, she should be checking on Arthur Bradley rather than Joe Spencer. At least she hadn't had to wrestle herself out of Joe's embrace, whereas Arthur had made a grab for her, practically forcing himself on her.

At the same time, she knew it would be unfair to speak her mind when she was angry, particularly after she had promised Arthur to say nothing of what had happened.

**PEGGY DARTY** is the popular, award-winning author of novels and magazine articles. Darty, who makes her home in Alabama, uses her extensive background in television and film to spin a tale of romance and intrigue that is sure to please all of her many fans.

**Books by Peggy Darty**

HEARTSONG PRESENTS
HP143—Morning Mountain
HP238—Song of the Dove
HP273—Summer Place

# Silent Stranger

*Peggy Darty*

Heartsong Presents

**A note from the author:**
*I love to hear from my readers! You may correspond with me
by writing:*      **Peggy Darty**
                  **Author Relations**
                  **PO Box 719**
                  **Uhrichsville, OH 44683**

**ISBN 1-57748-482-7**

**SILENT STRANGER**

All Scripture quotations are from the Authorized King James
Version of the Bible unless otherwise noted.

All of the characters and events in this book are fictitious. Any
resemblance to actual persons, living or dead, or to actual events
is purely coincidental.

*Cover illustration by Gary Maria.*

PRINTED IN THE U.S.A.

## one

Ruth Wright stepped from the general store onto the narrow boardwalk of Dawson in the Northwest Territories. Dawson had sprung up at the junction of the Yukon and Klondike Rivers soon after gold was discovered on Bonanza Creek, and the word had spread like wildfire across Canada, Alaska, and the United States since July 1897. Over the last year, people had poured into the territory—Ruth and her father included—and now the settlement had become a rowdy little town. Today Dawson was buzzing with excitement over the weekly arrival of a boat from "outside," for with the boat came mail, food, mining supplies, and news from all over the world.

Tucking a strand of auburn hair under her bonnet, she drew herself up to her five feet, seven inches and turned her slender body toward the wharf for she, too, was interested in the boat's arrival.

"Good afternoon, Ruth." Mrs. Greenwood stopped her. She was short, heavyset in middle age, and rumored to be the town gossip. "Who's at the clinic today?"

"It's been a quiet day, Mrs. Greenwood. Just a few routine calls. No major ailments." She took a secret delight in suppressing information from Mrs. Greenwood.

"Well, you and the doc better get ready! With all the new folks arriving, there'll be brawls in the street tonight."

Ruth glanced at her. "Maybe not."

Despite Mrs. Greenwood's negative opinion about the passengers, she joined Ruth in walking toward the dock, where the *Bella* was nudging its way into the shoreline. People

5

eagerly gathered up and down the shore watching.

"As usual, the men outnumber the women," Mrs. Greenwood said with a heavy sigh.

Ruth did not reply as she studied the strangers meandering tentatively down the gangplank. Watching, she tried to guess the professions of those arriving. It was easy to spot the miners—denim trousers, flannel shirts, felt hats. Then there were the men who had come to open shops; on their arms were women dressed in the fashion of the day.

"Hmmph," Mrs. Greenwood snorted. "They'll find out their city garb won't work here," she said as she and Ruth both stared at the fashionably high, stiff collars, narrow corseted waists, and wide bouffant skirts. "Look! Some of them are even wearing those disgraceful skirts!"

In cities, the fashion now was toward shorter skirts that showed the ankles.

"At least the knickers underneath will keep them warm," Ruth laughed, glad for her own. "Those were all the fad when I left Seattle."

"I call them bloomers," Mrs. Greenwood said under her breath. "I'm glad to see that not all of them are trying to be fashionmongers," she commented grudgingly. Mrs. Greenwood had gained ten pounds since Ruth had known her, and she couldn't help wonder if some of her criticism was due to her own dissatisfaction with herself.

"Reckon they'll be shedding those corsets soon enough," Mrs. Greenwood stated with pride. Automatically Ruth touched her waist, thinking how most of the women in Dawson had shed their corsets by mutual agreement, choosing comfort over fashion. It was difficult enough to keep the clothes clean and presentable, with having to deal with the mud of the streets and the occasional misfired stream of tobacco juice.

Ruth's eyes skimmed the crowd, recalling how she must have looked on the day she and her father arrived in June: She had worn her best silk dress with brush braid and interlined with buckram, which made the skirt swing wide when she walked.

An amused grin slipped over her full lips. She had worn the dress only once since her arrival nearly two months ago. At that time only those with money—like Ruth and her father, Dr. Wright, affectionately called Doc—could afford to arrive in Dawson City by boat. Many of the other inhabitants had come over the most difficult route, yet the cheapest. They had booked passage, one way or another, by steamer to Skagway, then struggled over the seven hundred miles to the Klondike by White Pass or Chilkoot Pass, each a challenge for human survival.

Somehow they had arrived, frostbitten, heavily bearded, and practically threadbare. They brought very little, having to shed their belongings piece by piece to lighten their load on the tortuous pass. When finally they stumbled in from the Klondike, thin as rails, many were in need of her father's medical attention. There was one other doctor in town, a fortyish widower by the name of Arthur Bradley, but Doc Wright's clinic was the busier one.

"Looks like the same kind of people," Mrs. Greenwood sighed.

As Ruth watched the boat's passengers disperse among the crowd, her eyes lingered on one young man in particular. He was tall with broad shoulders and long legs, and he wore the clothes of a laborer or a miner—denim trousers, red woolen shirt with long sleeves, and a black felt hat. She glimpsed thick, golden hair beneath the hat as he turned to speak with a huge, burly man beside him whose clothes were ragged and whose felt hat was smashed low on his forehead.

They had exited the gangplank and were now lost in the crowd.

"You heading home now?" Mrs. Greenwood asked as they turned back toward Front Street.

"Yes, actually I should have gone back sooner."

"And Mr. Greenwood will be wondering what's happened to me," she said, quickening her short steps. "I have to tell him about the boat."

Mrs. Greenwood was always on a mission for news. Her husband was one of the town assayers, and when Mrs. Greenwood ran low on conversation, he could pick up the slack. He knew the extent of everyone's wealth, particularly if their wealth came from gold dust or nuggets measured at his hands. He also knew which men were losing their shirts or had already busted and gone home. As it happened, the Greenwoods were Ruth's neighbors, which added to her discomfort. Her father merely seemed amused by the two.

As they parted company and Mrs. Greenwood turned down a side street to her husband's office, Ruth shifted the brown-papered bundle of supplies in her arms and hurried toward home. As she retraced her steps, she looked around her, wondering how the new arrivals aboard the *Bella* would regard Dawson. This was a town of white tents—most of them dirty by now—some hastily thrown up log dwellings, a few crude saloons, and a couple of hotels in various stages of development. Where there had once been a rough wilderness, the stampede for gold had brought thousands of people pouring into the territory. The screech of saws cutting across wood filled her ears as men worked day and night to construct dwellings. Every day brought a new adventure. It was the most exciting period of Ruth's twenty-one years.

Ruth had reached the end of the block and was now facing their two-story log house, the only two-story house in

Dawson. The first floor of the house was used for the clinic; the upstairs provided two bedrooms, a living room–dining room combination, and a kitchen. Her father had spared no expense when he commissioned the hasty building of the house before their arrival. He had paid dearly for the indoor toilet and well-insulated plumbing, but Ruth was eternally grateful. She couldn't bear to think of traipsing to the out-houses she saw behind most buildings. Her father felt by combining office and home, the luxury was warranted.

She noted there were no horses at the hitching rail, which could or could not indicate patients within the clinic. She climbed the porch steps of the simple log house and caught her breath. It had been a long walk and she was tired. Pausing at the horsehair mat, she scraped the mud from her rubber boots and opened the door.

Crossing the hall, she peered into the large front room of the clinic. The clinic was basically an office and a waiting room. An overstuffed sofa and table were balanced by several straight-backed chairs. Her father got up from behind his cluttered desk at the opposite end of the room and came to meet her.

"Has Dr. Bradley stolen your patients?" She looked around, teasing her father. "You must have cut off the wrong toe and Mrs. Greenwood got wind of it!"

Her father laughed, enjoying his daughter's humor. "Dr. Bradley is welcome to some of the load," he said, chuckling. "Here, let me help." He scooped the packages from her arms.

"The *Bella* just arrived," she said, removing her cape and placing it on the coat tree.

"I pray there was a generous amount of food for the merchants to stock their shelves," Doc was saying.

Ruth nodded as she looked at the tall man before her. Kind hazel eyes reflected the charm of his youth, but that youth had vanished with the death of Mary Ruth Wright three years ago and with the long work-filled days that had been so much a part of his life. Thick brows and dark lashes matched the darkness of his hair, although more gray than black now covered his head. His dark coat, superbly tailored, no longer concealed the paunch at his waist, but Ruth's smile merely widened. Her father enjoyed eating, and she loved cooking.

"Seriously, did anyone come by?" she asked, glancing around the clinic and noting that her father had already tidied things up. Her eyes lifted to the wooden bookcase that held numerous medical books and journals. One or two were askew, as though he had consulted them at some point during the day.

"Ned Joiner from the blacksmith shop. He got careless with the hammer and smashed his thumb. No permanent damage. All in all, I'd say it's been a rather dull day."

"Then I'm glad. You work too hard."

He was staring at her thoughtfully now. "Ruth, I couldn't manage without you. I hope you realize that."

"I do realize it. Besides, you don't take care of yourself very well. You need me to boss you around," she teased.

He chuckled. "Then I'll allow you to do that. But first, I'll take this package up to the kitchen for you."

"No, thank you." She wrestled the package from him. "You stretch out in the chair and put your feet up."

Strangely, he obeyed, tilting his head curiously at her as he took his seat.

"Why are you looking at me that way?" she asked frankly.

He smiled. "It's just that you remind me so much of your beautiful mother—the auburn hair, the heart-shaped face, the way you move and talk and think."

"Thank you," she replied, touched by the compliment. Her mother was the kindest person she had ever known and, like her father, Ruth had been devastated by her death.

"But I have your eyes," she reminded him, and they both laughed. "Well, I must start supper."

She climbed the steps to their apartment on the second floor. Entering the living room, her eyes moved over the simple wooden furniture they had purchased from local carpenters. It was a far cry from the fine pieces they had left behind, but in Dawson City, everyone had to start all over again.

She hurried to the kitchen, depositing her goods on the cabinet. The kitchen always gave her a sense of contentment, perhaps because in Seattle the kitchen had been the center of their family life. Her mother loved to cook and had dispensed with kitchen help, even though most families of their status hired cooks and maids. The only concession her mother made was hiring a cleaning lady for their large home. The kitchen belonged to Ruth and her mother. Unable to conceive another child after Ruth, her mother had tried to make up for their small family by constantly entertaining.

The sound of horse hooves outside brought her to the window. She parted the muslin curtain and peered down. Her eyes widened. To her surprise, the man she had spotted on the gangplank of the *Bella* was slowly getting down from a brown sorrel with a well-tended harness. Yes, it was him—and now she could see that he was even taller as her eyes scanned the long legs that stretched to brown cowhide boots. His red shirt strained against well-toned muscles as he hitched his horse at the log rail. Then suddenly his eyes moved upward to the window where she stood gawking.

Ruth stepped back, realizing she shouldn't be so judgmental of Mrs. Greenwood, for at the moment she was burning with curiosity. She heard his knock, and then her father's steps crossed the hall to the front door. She walked to the open door and stood listening.

"I'm Doc Wright." Her father's voice floated up to her.

"I'm Joe Spencer," he said, speaking slowly. "I hurt my back down at the dock just now. Thought I should get it checked."

"Then come in and let's have a look."

Ruth could hear them crossing the hall, and then the clinic door closed. She supposed if her father needed her, he would call for her. She stopped at the counter, picking up a narrow black satin ribbon. Suddenly conscious of the wispy strands of auburn hair dangling at her collar, she gripped the ribbon with her teeth and swept her hair back from her face, securing it at the nape of her neck with the ribbon.

Her curiosity about the man downstairs lingered as she rolled up the long sleeves of her blouse. He was a southerner; she could tell from his accent.

She rinsed her hands in the wash pan, wondering if he had seriously injured his back; from the way he moved, she would guess it was a strain. She dried her hands on a cup towel then turned to check the dough she had left rising near the stove. As she pressed her thumb into the fat dough and made a fingerprint, she reached for the rolling pin. Scrambled eggs with biscuits and a tin of molasses settled the question of supper. How could she manage an invitation to the stranger? Or was he married? Her heart sank. Probably.

The door opened again, and she heard her father speaking. "Just apply that liniment and don't lift anything heavy. If you want to stop in tomorrow, I'll have a larger bottle. Some of my medical supplies should have come in on the boat. Say, want to come up and have a cup of coffee?"

There was a moment's hesitation while she grabbed the teakettle.

"If it's no bother."

"No bother at all. We drink a lot of coffee here," he was

saying as the men climbed the stairs.

Ruth had poured hot water from the teakettle into the tin coffeepot and now had it back on the stove. She was spooning coffee grounds into the pot as their footsteps entered the living room. "Have a seat," her father was saying. "You need to bend your knees and ease yourself slowly onto the sofa. Protect that back." Doc poked his head around the door. "Could we—"

"I'm making coffee," she said, smiling at him.

"Thank you." He grinned then turned back to the living room.

"How long have you been here, Doc?" The smooth voice of the stranger drifted to her.

"My daughter and I came up from Seattle in June. I'd spent my life there. After the Panic in '93, the country was in a depression. It seemed the Pacific Northwest was especially slow to recover. Many of my patients couldn't even pay their medical bills, but I wouldn't turn them away. They were people I'd known for years."

Listening from the kitchen, Ruth nodded, thinking about how tenderhearted her father had always been. She checked to be sure the water was boiling then grabbed tall mugs from the cupboard.

"When the *Portland* steamed into Seattle last year—July 17 it was—with news of the Klondike gold strike, Seattle went crazy. Salespeople bolted over the counters; firemen and policemen threw down their uniforms; even the mayor resigned. I heard that one preacher walked out on his congregation!"

Both men laughed at that, and from the kitchen Ruth listened, enjoying the sound of Joe Spencer's laughter. Everything about this stranger fascinated her.

"San Francisco was much the same way," Joe replied.

"I think everyone was hungry for change," Doc continued. "The idea of gold and adventure appealed to all of us. I heard the Yukon was desperate for doctors, so my daughter and I left as soon as we could have our place built. But then, after all I'd heard about the Klondike and its thriving towns, Ruth and I were pretty disappointed when we got here. From the boat this place just looked like one big swamp sprawled along a riverbank." He chuckled.

"I reckon the first settlers here had a real vision about what the town could become," Joe said. "It seems to be thriving now."

"Yes, it is," Doc agreed. "And you're right, Joe Ladue had a real vision when he put up a warehouse and a sawmill. He knew what he was doing, that's for sure. My biggest gripe with Dawson, I guess, is those who try to get rich on the settlers."

"Yes, sir. I'd heard men complain about how the merchants had tripled the prices on everything. When I went into the mercantile this afternoon, I almost dropped the sack of sec- ondhand nails when the clerk priced them at eight dollars a pound."

"It's ridiculous," Doc replied, his voice filled with contempt.

"As a matter of fact, sir, you have the best price in town for services rendered."

"Thank you. That's a nice thing to say. I just came to help, that's all."

"The people here are fortunate you made that decision, Dr. Wright."

"Just call me Doc. Everyone does."

"Do you dabble in mining at all, Doc?"

Her father hesitated. As Ruth pulled the coffeepot from the burner, she wondered if her father would admit that he owned a claim. A half-starved miner had collapsed on their doorstep while waiting for the next boat out. In payment for services, he had given Doc the claim, which appeared useless and had nearly killed him.

"I don't have time to think about mining." Doc sidestepped the question. "I'm not inclined to hire someone to build a shaft down into the earth or wade through the frozen streams in winter. And I certainly don't want to do that."

"I feel sure you'll end up with more money in this profession," the stranger said.

Ruth stared at the thin curl of smoke drifting up from the spout of the coffeepot, suffusing her pale cheeks with color. *Keep talking*, she silently pleaded. She loved his accent.

Her father peered around the door, glancing at the coffeepot.

"It's ready," she said.

"Ruth, won't you come in and join us?" He walked over to get the tray from the cupboard.

Her eyes darted to him then back to the mugs. "All right."

Placing the mugs on a tray, along with spoons and sugar, she followed her father into the living room. The tray was a far cry from her mother's silver service she had used so many times; a silver service in Dawson City would be subject to theft, not to mention the fact that it would look oddly out of place.

Joe Spencer stood as she entered, almost startling her with his good manners. She placed the tray on the coffee table then straightened, dropping her hands to her sides.

"Mr. Spencer, this is my daughter, Ruth Wright."

"How do you do?" she said, smiling at him.

"Hello." He nodded politely. "Thank you for the coffee."

"We don't have cream," she said, glancing back at the tray.

"I drink it black. Since coming north, I've learned to be happy with the bare necessities. It suits me fine." He spoke with confidence as his eyes lingered on Ruth. She turned to the tray.

"And where is home for you?" Doc asked, leaning back on the sofa, studying him thoughtfully.

"Richmond, Virginia," he said. "Thank you." His eyes met Ruth's as she handed him a mug of coffee.

His eyes were a clear, bright blue. He had thick brown brows and darker brown lashes, a slim straight nose, full lips, and a square chin. He was unquestionably the most handsome man she had seen in a very long time. If ever. She turned and handed her father his coffee, then took her mug and sat in the nearest chair, studying Joe Spencer over her mug.

"How did you get all the way to Dawson from Richmond?" Doc asked curiously.

"I went to California five years ago at the invitation of my uncle, who was working on a ranch out from San Francisco. I enjoyed the life of a cowhand for a few years, but after my uncle died, I left the ranch and went into San Francisco looking for work. I heard about the Klondike strike and decided I wanted to give it a try. So I worked as a carpenter and saved every cent I made until I could board the ship."

"You were wise to choose the ship rather than trying to cross Chilkoot Pass on foot as so many are doing."

Joe Spencer shook his head. "I had already heard horror stories about that route. A fellow I worked with at the lumber yard joined some guys who were going up in '96. He almost died trying to get over the pass. He turned around and came home with tuberculosis and an amputated foot due to frostbite."

Doc nodded. "I fear we're in for a winter of such maladies." He paused, glancing over at Ruth. Then his eyes returned to Joe Spencer. "Did you come alone?" he asked.

Ruth glanced at her father, thinking he was almost as curious as she was about this stranger with the southern accent.

"I did, but I've made friends. In fact, one of my friends, Ivan Bertoff, will be going out to the mining district with me when I leave tomorrow." His eyes drifted slowly to Ruth.

"How do you like living here, Miss Wright?" he asked.

Surprised by his question, she swallowed the hot coffee too quickly and almost choked. She kept her composure, however, as she licked her lips and looked at him. "I like it."

"It must seem quite a change from Seattle," he said as his eyes drifted over her face.

She reached up to push a lock of auburn hair back from her forehead. "It is, but I enjoy the satisfaction of helping others. My father is a wonderful doctor."

"I've already benefitted from his services." He finished his coffee and came slowly to his feet. "I've imposed for long enough. I must get busy gathering the supplies I'll need. What time would you like me to come in tomorrow?"

Doc shrugged. "We don't make appointments here. It's first come, first serve."

Joe laughed. "Then I'll see you in the morning." He turned to Ruth. "It was a pleasure meeting you."

Their eyes locked and Ruth felt something strange and different as she looked at Joe Spencer, something she had never felt before. "Thank you," she said.

He turned and nodded at Doc then headed for the door, hat in hand. Doc followed him back down the stairs as Ruth returned to the kitchen, trying to sort out her feelings. He had told them very little about himself. He hadn't mentioned a wife, but how could a man so handsome reach—at least thirty years of age she guessed—and remain single?

❧

Joe Spencer tried to ignore the ache in his back as he weaved his way through the crowd. Glancing around, he recognized some of the boat passengers, but many of the men on the street were obviously miners. With tanned faces and thick beards, they wore tattered clothing and surveyed the newly arriving people through narrowed eyes.

He kept thinking of the Wrights and feeling a sense of regret that he wouldn't allow himself to get to know them better. But he had to be careful; already, he worried he had told them too much. Still, there was something about them that made him feel at home and comfortable; he longed to enjoy their hospitality, take advantage of their kindness. But he would be taking advantage and he knew that; he could stay nowhere for long. The secrets in his past dogged him like predators; memories howled like the wolves on a cold night, and he had spent many cold nights alone in the woods, listening to the wolves howl.

Joe located the Bank of British North America, which was actually a large tent with a board plank for a counter and an old trunk for a safe—both proof of how new Dawson City was. Joe's eyes widened. Around the trunk, Joe spotted several sacks of gold on the sawdust floor.

He reached deep into the pocket of his denim trousers and withdrew a deerskin bag of gold dust. He offered the bag to the assayer, wanting to convert some of his gold dust to cash for a deposit in the bank. For spending money, the common practice was to use gold dust. When an impressive sum had been opened in his account, he thanked the clerk and left.

Just down the street he spotted the Alaska Commercial Company and entered. The store was a large, square room filled with shoppers milling about the counter, which ran the length of one side. Although the days were still long and the air was crisp but not cold, the potbellied stove in the corner held a low fire. Two well-dressed men from the boat were conversing with three miners, each hungry for news the other had to offer. Joe turned toward the shelves, consulting the list he pulled from the pocket of his shirt, and began to stack up the items: sugar, flour, salt, canned milk, beans, tea. He added a hefty slab of bacon then paused, glancing toward another array of shelves. Consulting his list again, he walked over to select a pick, shovel, and a metal pan. What other tools did he need? He frowned, trying to concentrate despite the boisterous crowd.

Joe had been forced to leave his other supplies behind in Skagway, but he had brought what he needed most: the gold dust. He turned to the cashier and slowly withdrew another deerskin bag from the pocket of his denim trousers. He handed the bag to the clerk and waited; as he did, his eyes made a slow, careful sweep of the room. There were no familiar faces; Ivan still had not appeared.

The clerk weighed the gold dust on scales positioned on a thick, black velvet cloth. Joe wondered how much gold dust ended up on that cloth by the end of the day. He watched the scales tip and noted the look of surprise on the clerk's face. The man cast his eyes over the crowd and leaned toward Joe. "About ninety dollars," he whispered.

Joe nodded. "Will you total my supplies and see if this is enough?"

Joe knew it would be. If not, there was another pouch of gold dust, but he needed that to survive through the winter.

"Could you tell me where I could obtain some good dogs?" he asked the clerk while the man packaged up his supplies.

"Try Arvin Christensen. His place is on the south end of town, first road to the right. Has a white banner in his yard advertising his business."

"Thanks," Joe said. "And what about a place to stay?"

"Try Mattie's Roadhouse. It's the best we have to offer until the hotel is completed. She's down at the south end, too, but you better hurry. With the boat coming in, she may be filled up already."

"Thanks again," he said.

His good luck was still holding when he obtained the last

cot in the boardinghouse. The log structure was actually four large rooms with as many cots as Mattie could cram into each room. For the ladies who had accompanied their men, another room awaited them. This room was strictly for males, and already six were sprawled on the cots, snoring loudly.

Joe pushed his supplies up under the cot and hesitated, wondering if it would be safe to leave them while he checked on the dogs. The ache in his back had intensified after carrying the load, and he could no longer pass up the cot. The dogs could wait, he decided, as he removed his boots and stretched out on the cot.

When he closed his eyes, he saw Ruth Wright, and this surprised him. He had been impressed by her beauty—the fair skin that was enhanced even more by thick auburn hair and deep hazel eyes. And yet it was the depth he sensed in the woman that drew him even more. She had to be brave and adventurous—and unselfish—to accompany her father here to the frozen north. She obviously had no idea what was in store for her. No doubt, she would be on the first boat when spring breakup came and there was boat travel again.

It didn't matter, he told himself. He had a plan, and no woman would fit into his plan. Not ever again.

# two

Ruth and Doc shared their simple meal in relative silence in the glow of the lantern. Doc had been in the process of buttering a biscuit when suddenly he laid down his knife and looked across the small table. "I hope the winter here won't be too harsh for you. We haven't yet experienced the cold and—"

She put up her hand. "Father, I am no longer the forgetful young girl who dashes off without mittens or muff. I find Dawson exciting. And I'm very proud of what you're doing here. Like you, I'm far more interested in seeing a sick person restored to good health than sitting by a cozy fire in Seattle, pricking my thumb with a needle."

He sighed, leaning back in the wooden chair. "We're going to have some gruesome illnesses to treat. Frostbitten hands and feet, consumption, scurvy, perhaps even tuberculosis."

"Please." She pressed a hand to her stomach. "I'm trying to enjoy my meal."

"Sorry." He grinned, acknowledging her mock humor. "Do you think we have enough food to last the winter?" he asked suddenly.

"You are determined to be a worrywart, aren't you?" she gently scolded.

His brow was creased with concern as he glanced toward the wooden shelves behind the pantry curtain.

"We can't crowd one more item on those shelves, Father. I'd say we could live comfortably for two years!"

He sighed. "It's just that once the Yukon freezes over, which will be soon, there will be no more boats coming in. We'll be cut off from the outside world. There'll be no—"

"Father, I'm not worried," she said quickly, wanting to turn his thoughts in another direction. "If a stocked pantry had been of primary importance, I would have married William Manchester and grown fat and bored with him."

He did not laugh, as she had expected. He merely stared at her for a moment, as though trying to be certain she meant what she was saying.

She tilted her head and stared at him. "Why won't you believe that I really wanted to come here? That I didn't make the trip just for you?"

Slowly, a weary smile tilted his lips and some of the age in his face faded. "I want to believe that. But I keep thinking that you didn't want to hold me back; you knew I wouldn't leave you behind unmarried. And if you wouldn't marry William—"

"Father." She threw down her napkin as her temper began to flare. "William Manchester may have been considered attractive and well educated by a lot of Seattle women, but I did not love him. And I knew I never would. I want to feel what you and Mother felt for one another." She bit her lip, lost in thought.

Tears glistened in her father's hazel eyes before he quickly lowered his head. "I pray that you will have that someday," he said quietly. "To be truthful, I will never get over losing your mother. This adventure to the Klondike has been good for me, but I still long for Mary Ruth every day of my life."

She swallowed hard and her temper vanished as quickly as it had appeared. "I miss her, too, Father, but we have to go on. We're doing a good work here, a Christian service to these people, which must please Mother to no end. You know she is watching from heaven," she added softly, thinking she would read from her mother's Bible at bedtime.

"Yes," he said, unashamedly wiping the tears from his eyes. "And I'm glad you didn't marry William if you didn't love him."

"I didn't. He was aggressive, overpowering, and opinionated. I'll tell you something else, which I hope will end this discussion once and for all. I was certain that William would miss the benefits of his clubs and social events more than he would miss me; still, I decided to put him to the test. I told him if he really loved me, I'd like him to accompany us to the Klondike. I even promised to return with him in a year. He was quick to agree with me that this was not the life for him. So you see, if he had really loved me, he wouldn't have backed down so easily."

Doc nodded. "You're absolutely right." Something flashed in his eyes as he studied her face. "What did you think of Joe Spencer?"

She fought the color rising on her cheeks, telegraphing her feelings. "I don't know him, so how could I make a judgment?" She got up from the table, clearing away the dishes.

Her father stood, too, chuckling softly.

"Why are you laughing?" She whirled on him.

"I just had an amusing thought, that's all. I'm going downstairs to look through one of the new journals that came in by boat."

With that, he had disappeared, leaving her to her thoughts. She stared at the fluffy biscuits remaining in the pan and thought of Joe Spencer. What was he doing at this hour? Was he at the Bonanza Saloon like so many other men? Or was he already settled in someplace for the night?

After cleaning the kitchen, she picked up the mug that she had set apart from the others, the mug that Joe Spencer had held. Her slim fingers traced the round curve of the mug, relishing the thought that his lips had touched the enameled surface. Shaking herself back to reality, she quickly put the mug in the cabinet and went to her bedroom.

As she undressed and prepared for bed, she picked up her mother's Bible and turned the wick up on the lantern. She opened the Bible to Psalm 119, which had been one of her mother's favorites. Her eyes skimmed down the verses and lingered on those she had marked.

"Thy word have I hid in mine heart, that I might not sin
   against thee.
Blessed art thou, O Lord: teach me thy statutes.
With my lips have I declared all the judgments of thy
   mouth.
I have rejoiced in the way of thy testimonies, as much as
   in all riches.
I will meditate in thy precepts, and have respect unto thy
   ways.
I will delight myself in thy statutes: I will not forget thy
   word.
Deal bountifully with thy servant, that I may live, and
   keep thy word.
Open thou mine eyes, that I may behold wondrous
   things out of thy law."

Ruth paused, staring at the next verse, which seemed so appropriate for her.

"I am a stranger in the earth: hide not thy command-
   ments from me."

She stopped reading and stared into space. She was a stranger to this country, to this way of life. There were times she felt frightened by that, although she would never admit as much to her father. But now this verse had given her comfort. She knew the word of God. She had grown up at her mother's knee, having the Bible read to her. It had always been a source of comfort to her, and just reading the verses from her mother's Bible tonight had given her such peace and joy.

She closed the Bible and smiled to herself, basking in the radiance of God's love.

Ruth returned the Bible to the nightstand and blew softly into the globe, extinguishing the flame. Snuggling deeper under the quilts, she closed her eyes and said her prayers. Her last thought before she drifted into sleep was that she was more grateful than ever that she had not married William Manchester.

❧

The next morning Ruth took extra care as she chose a favorite green dress of soft wool topped by the fashionably high, stiff collar. She even resorted to her corset today, for the special liniment her father had ordered had been delivered last night. When Joe Spencer came to their clinic, her father would check his back and apply the liniment again. And she wanted to look appealing. She had been grateful to learn that Joe had paid cash for her father's services. That was always a relief.

Her father was willing to take anything as payment from his patients, ranging from a sick dog to a lame mule. This held true regardless of how many times he had seen the patient or the extent of his care for that patient. The next needy miner who came to his door would more than likely be the recipient of the dog or mule. Failing all else, he even wrote No Charge on certain charts. He was a good Christian man, unable to turn a needy soul from their door.

The temperature had dropped below freezing in the night, and her fingers were stiff with cold as she fumbled for a ribbon. Tossing her auburn hair back from her face, she gathered it into one thick mass. She slipped the ribbon under her hair and pulled it tight, tying it into a bow at the nape of her neck.

Her father was an early riser, and he had left coffee for her on the stove. She had covered the leftover biscuits from last night, and now she plucked one from the pan, enjoying its fluffy taste. She poured herself a mug of coffee and sat down at the table, trying to organize her thoughts. It was not yet eight, and there were no patients downstairs, so she devoted her energy to preparing a stew that could simmer in the Dutch oven until lunch. Her potato stew was usually good, so she went to the cabinet, jammed with food, and retrieved some potatoes and located a paring knife. Humming to herself, she went to work.

ðª

Joe Spencer had decided to wait another day before heading into the hills. He had slept comfortably on the cot and was pleased to learn that Mattie could be trusted. She had agreed to lock his supplies in her bedroom closet, freeing him up to do more shopping today and stop off at Doc Wright's clinic one last time.

His first mission was to check out the dogs. He didn't have to have a sled and dogs to carry supplies, but it would be good if he could find what he needed at the right price. He headed for the place he had been told about the day before. It was easy to follow the sound of dogs barking as he sloshed through the mud where the boardwalk ended, making his way to the log house where a white banner in the front yard advertised Malamutes For Sale.

A tall bearded man in denim trousers and a red flannel shirt stood in the front yard, surveying the sky.

"Hello," Joe called. "I wanted to see your dogs."

"How many?" the man asked, looking him over.

Joe hesitated, uncertain. "I don't know yet. Also, do you have a sled for sale?"

"Matter of fact, I do." The man motioned him around the side of the house to the backyard. Enclosed in a log fence were four brown and white malamutes, along with four other dogs of mixed breed. All appeared to be in good health.

"Man just sold me his sled and the eight dogs there. The dogs are well trained. They can pull a load for eight hours."

Joe frowned. "That's a long time."

"And a heavy load, too," the man said, ignoring the sympathy in Joe's voice.

Joe studied the dogs, pleased to see that their coats were lush, well tended, their eyes bright. He had always had a soft spot in his heart for dogs.

"How much for the sled and dogs?" He turned back to the man.

"Two thousand."

Joe stared at him. "That's ridiculous."

The man shrugged. "I'll get that much, perhaps more as winter sets in."

Joe sighed, tallying up his money. Even though he had a comfortable nest egg, he was not going to submit to such an exorbitant price. He cast another glance toward the dogs, regretting that he was unable to purchase them.

"How much does it take to feed those dogs?" he asked curiously.

"Man said he gave them lots of fish and maybe a thousand pounds of bacon over a year's time."

Joe whistled. "That's better than I'll be eating," he said wryly. "Can't afford them," he said and turned to leave. Then another thought occurred to him. "What about one dog? Do you have just one good malamute for sale?"

This took the man by surprise. "One dog can't pull much."

"No, but he could be a good companion."

"I've got a good male over here." He led Joe around to another enclosure where a brown and white malamute with soft brown eyes won Joe's heart at first sight. Joe leaned down to rub the top of his brown head and study the white muzzle of fur around his eyes and mouth.

"He's twenty-six inches at the shoulders, weighs seventy-four pounds," Christensen announced.

Joe checked out the white underside of the dog's body and the sturdy white legs. He appeared to be a strong, healthy dog, and he was a friendly one, licking at Joe's hand. Joe's eyes skimmed over the brown back to the white tail curled over his back. He looked back at the almond-shaped eyes, filled with soul, and couldn't resist. "I'll take him," he said, without asking the price.

An hour later, with his new malamute leading the way, Joe gripped the leash and headed toward Doc's clinic.

❧

Ruth listened to her father's lecture on vitamin C to Lucky Herndon, a local miner who was a frequent patient. The nickname Lucky had been a cruel joke on someone's part for the thin, bedraggled man seemed always in a streak of bad luck. Today he had come in complaining of aching muscles and showing bruises on his skin. Lucky was dressed as usual in patched denims, faded gray shirt, and dirt-encrusted boots. Doc had checked him over and assessed the bruises on his skin. Then he had looked in his mouth and shaken his head at Lucky's bleeding gums.

"You've got scurvy, Lucky," Doc said with a sigh.

"Scurvy?" Lucky croaked. Nervously, he removed his battered gray hat and raked through his thin hair that overlapped his collar. His long face seemed to lengthen as the jaw sagged. "That's bad news, ain't it?"

"Could be worse. How long you been without fruit?" Doc asked, closing his black bag.

Lucky shook his head. "I can't remember."

"Well, let me tell you something, Lucky. Don't even think about going back to that claim until you go to the store and get some decent food in your system. Ruth, do we have any oranges left?"

Ruth nodded and went upstairs to the pantry. Oranges were selling for one dollar each, and she doubted the poor man could afford them. There were half a dozen on their shelf, so she removed half of them and headed back downstairs. When she returned, her father was giving him a bottle of pills.

Just then the front door opened, and she turned to see Joe Spencer, who had just stepped into the hall. Her heart jumped at the sight of him, and she wondered what she was going to do about these crazy feelings she was experiencing each time she saw the man.

"Hello." He smiled at her.

"Hello." She smiled back.

"Want to see my new dog?" he asked her.

"Sure," she said then laughed.

It was a surprising question, but she followed him out to the front porch, where a handsome malamute sat, surveying the surroundings. She knelt, stroking his thick fur. "Hi there," she said then glanced up at Joe. "What's his name?"

"I'm going to call him Kenai," he answered.

She lifted a brow. "Kenai?"

He shrugged then propped a broad shoulder against the door jamb. "After a beautiful peninsula."

"That's a nice name," she said as she continued to stroke the dog's fur, yet her eyes had never left Joe's face.

Ruth held his gaze for a few more seconds. He was wearing fresh clothes—another pair of denim trousers, a brown wool shirt, and matching hat. He was clean-shaven, unlike so many she had seen.

The door behind him opened and the miner stumbled out, holding a sack.

"Now take your medicine and eat those oranges," Doc warned. "Come back and see me next week."

"Thanks, Doc." His faded blue eyes swept Doc then Ruth. "Thanks, ma'am."

"You're welcome." Ruth stood, brushing her hands.

"Nice dog," Doc said, glancing down. "How's your back, Spencer?"

"Better. A decent bed helped," Joe added as he and Ruth followed Doc back inside.

Ruth noticed as they entered the hall that the scent of the potato stew wafted pleasantly over the downstairs. She wanted to invite Joe to lunch, but she felt it was her father's place to do that.

"Father, I'm going to check on lunch. It will be ready soon," she added.

He nodded then looked at Joe. "Want to stay and join us? I'd like to hear more about San Francisco."

Joe glanced at Ruth as she lifted her skirts to climb the stairs. "Yes, sir, I'd be pleased to stay if it's not an imposition."

She glanced back over her shoulder. "No, it isn't."

ès

Later, as the three of them sat around the kitchen table, Ruth tried to conceal the joy she felt over having Joe with them. She could hardly keep her eyes from his handsome face, and he seemed to be looking her way a lot.

She lifted the platter of corn bread and offered him a slice.

"Thank you," he said. Again, his eyes lingered on her face for a fraction of a second.

"So," her father spoke up, "we were going to talk about San

Francisco. I haven't been there in years. What's it like now?"

"The people are depressed over the money situation, the same way you mentioned folks are in Seattle. When news of the gold strike here reached the city, it caused a major upheaval. Everyone quit their jobs and tried to book passage on the first boat out."

He paused for a sip of coffee.

"I finally got passage on an old coal tanker and had the pleasure of breathing coal dust all the way to Skagway. Seemed like where there was space for one man, four were crammed in. In fact, there were about eight hundred people on that old clunker."

"And you got off in Skagway?"

"I did, along with a lot of other people waiting for another ship going farther north. If your clinic was located there, you would have been in business night and day," Joe added then searched his mind for another topic to quickly change the subject. "What do you treat most people for here, Dr. Wright?"

Doc dipped in his stew again. "Scurvy. I imagine it will soon be frostbite when the harsh winter sets in." He looked up at Joe. "If you don't have a hot water bottle, that would be a good investment. Mrs. Mulrooney sells them at her roadhouse on the edge of town. She was smart to think of bringing hot water bottles to sell." He winked at his daughter. "Ruth, why didn't you think of that?"

Ruth got up to refill the coffee cups. "You didn't give me a lot of time to think of hot water bottles," she replied lightly.

꙳

Joe watched Ruth and her father, admiring the way they got along together. He had been without family for a very long time, and he found himself drawn to the doctor and his daughter—particularly the daughter—in a way that could prove dangerous for him. He concentrated on his food, trying to goad himself into leaving as soon as it would be polite to do so.

"Father, what's wrong?" Ruth had asked.

He looked up. Doc's face had turned gray, and for a moment, he said nothing.

"Do you have some food caught in your throat?" she asked, hurrying to his side.

Joe stood, staring down at the man, wondering what he could do. But then Doc shook his head and took a deep breath. "Just a slight case of indigestion, I think." He pushed his plate back and looked at his daughter. "You feed me too well."

Joe watched him carefully, noticing that the color had not returned to his face, although his smile and the pleasant hazel eyes seemed to convince his daughter. Narrowing his eyes, Joe studied him for another moment. He was a doctor; he, of all people, should know if something were wrong, and he claimed to have indigestion. Something nagged at Joe, however; something he could not pinpoint. Then he remembered. He had seen that gray color last year on the face of an older gentleman before he toppled onto the saloon table and died.

"I didn't prepare a dessert," she said, a note of apology in her voice.

Joe shook his head. "I don't care for sweets, but thank you. As a matter of fact, I really should get on with my errands, although I feel it's impolite to eat and leave."

"It's quite all right," she said. Then she turned to Joe and startled him senseless with her next statement. "We attend midweek prayer services tonight. Would you like to join us?"

Joe's mind raced. How could he pretend he was leaving town tonight when he had admitted a few minutes ago that he was departing at first light tomorrow? And at the moment, he couldn't even think of an excuse not to join them. He glanced quickly at her father. The man's color still was not good, and Joe found himself filled with concern for another individual for the first time in a year.

"We would like that," her father added seriously.

Joe touched the soft napkin to his lips, still searching his mind for an excuse and still finding none. "Where are the services held?" he asked.

"Up on the north end of town," Doc replied, "next to the tent that advertises blankets for sale. Services are held in one of the few clean white tents in Dawson. At the present, it's the only church we have, such as it is, but by next year there will be a building on that spot."

Joe nodded, feeling the pull of Ruth's eyes. He could see that she wanted him to join them, and for some reason he didn't understand, he decided to go.

"All right, thank you for inviting me." He hesitated then decided to be truthful. "I used to be a Christian—"

"Used to be?" Ruth tilted her head and gazed at him with questioning eyes.

He shifted uncomfortably. "Well, I still am. What I meant was, I was raised to attend church, but I haven't gone in. . . quite a while. If my mother were alive, she would be grateful to you for inviting me." His voice softened at the mention of his mother. Nothing in his life had been the same since she died.

He pushed back his chair. "I have some errands to run this afternoon. What time do services start?"

"We start early," Doc replied. "Six this evening. The preacher works days at the docks, so he's usually too tired to be long-winded."

Joe smiled, coming to his feet. He looked at Ruth again. "Thank you for a nice meal." He looked back at Doc, relieved to see that the color was returning to his face. He looked normal again. Maybe it was only indigestion, after all. "And thank you for treating my back. Oh," he reached into his pocket, "I forgot to pay you today."

Doc shook his head. "You paid yesterday. This was just a follow-up visit. And the pleasure of your company has been payment enough. See you tonight."

Joe hesitated. "Very well. Thanks for inviting me," he added, glancing at Ruth.

"By the way," Ruth said, going to the cabinet, "I have something for Kenai." She handed him a small bowl of left-overs. "You can keep the bowl," she added with a smile.

He stared into the oval face, mesmerized by the way her deep auburn hair made her skin look as soft as cream, and the eyes were a hazel color that was quite unusual. Joe wished he had the time to get to know her, to give over to the feelings that were nudging at his heart. But he didn't. He took the bowl from her and smiled. "Kenai will be grateful," he said.

They said their good-byes and Joe hurried down the stairs to the hall, bowl in hand. He thought about what nice people the Wrights were and how he wished he had met them a year ago. If he had, his life might have been drastically different. But he had not. And he had to live with the man he had become.

# three

Ruth and her father had chosen a seat on the middle bench, with her father seated next to the aisle. The crowd was sparse tonight, despite the arrival of the boat, which should have added to the small congregation. In contrast, the saloons were livelier than usual, having absorbed many of the boat's passengers.

Inside the tent that served as their church, the minister, Grant Sprayberry, stood at the front of the benches, Bible in hand, ready to conduct the service. He led the songs, as well. There were no musical instruments, so it was fortunate for everyone that he had a strong voice and an ear for music. Since there were no hymnals, he took requests for favorite hymns. First, he asked if anyone was in need of special prayer. Ruth vaguely heard the requests, lowered her head during prayer time, and tried to join in mentally.

Still, this was difficult, because Ruth was beginning to feel anxious. She and her father had waited outside the tent for Joe until time for the service, but he had not appeared. Doc had made an excuse for him, but Ruth was embarrassed and humiliated by his failure to show up. How could he eat their meal, accept their kindness, then be so rude? Was it possible that something had come up? She remembered his hesitation when she first invited him, and now she suspected that he had not wanted to come but was reluctant to refuse. So he had taken the easy way out.

"What's our song for tonight?" Pastor Sprayberry asked.

"How about 'Rock of Ages'?" someone in the rear of the church called out.

"'Rock of Ages' it is." Pastor Sprayberry smiled. He was a tall, middle-aged man with a wife and two daughters. When the pastor smiled, his entire face lit up, and he was smiling now.

Ruth tried to recall the verses to the hymn, since most hymns were sung by memory.

*Rock of ages, cleft for me, Let me hide myself in thee. . .*

"Excuse me."

She turned to see Joe Spencer standing in the aisle beside her father.

Doc nodded and Joe stepped in front of him, attempting to slip quietly past Ruth to fill the empty space on the other side of her.

"Sorry I'm late," he whispered.

She merely smiled and began to sing the hymn. All voices were lifted joyfully in praise, and while Joe did not open his mouth to sing, he seemed to be standing very still beside her.

After three verses of the hymn, the pastor opened his Bible and began to read from Psalms. He had chosen a favorite Psalm—the Twenty-third—and most people seemed to know it by heart, as they read along with him.

Ruth was holding her mother's Bible, and she shared the open page with Joe. He did not take a corner of the Bible; he merely followed the verses with his eyes. Then the pastor began to speak about the journey of life, emphasizing the importance of having the Lord as our shepherd, taking each verse and relating it to life's daily journey. When he had finished the simple, yet heartwarming message, he took requests for another hymn.

Doc Wright spoke up. "Amazing Grace."

Ruth smiled sadly. It was her mother's favorite hymn, and she and her father had always liked it, as well.

*Amazing grace! How sweet the sound, That saved a wretch like me. . .*

She lifted her voice in song, feeling joy stir through her soul.

*I once was lost, but now am found, Was blind, but now I see.*

At the end of the first stanza, she glanced at Joe. Quickly, her eyes flew back to the front of the tent where Grant Sprayberry stood. She didn't want to make Joe self-conscious by having him know she had seen him in a vulnerable moment. But there was no mistaking it; he had tears in his eyes.

❧

Joe swallowed hard, lowered his eyes, and hoped that Ruth had not seen the emotion that seemed to be flooding through him. What was wrong with him? First, the woman beside him had turned his head since he first met her. Being near her left him feeling as though he wanted to stand at her side for. . . well, for a long time. Now, he was reacting to the message, to the hymns, to the simple words the man had spoken. Well, he couldn't react, he couldn't feel anything. Not now; most of all, *not now.*

He concentrated on his hands, on the long fingers laced together before him. He thought of the mining claim, how rich he would be. He even forced himself to remember the cute little gal he had met in Skagway, although he couldn't even remember her name.

"We are so glad you could come." The soft voice beside him pulled his thoughts back to the moment. He turned and looked at her. She had tilted her head back to look at him, and her hazel eyes sparkled in a way that made his heart beat faster.

He cleared his throat, trying to summon back the manners his mother had taught him growing up. "Thank you for inviting me," he responded.

He looked over her head and saw that people were leaving

now; it was his chance to get out, and he was eager to do that. He could feel her eyes lingering on his face for another few seconds, but he didn't look back at her. He pretended an interest in the people who had attended the service, but in truth, it didn't matter.

"Glad you could join us." Doc extended his hand for a shake.

"Thank you. I'm sorry I was late." He glanced quickly at Ruth then turned back to her father. "My partner wants to leave Dawson this evening, so I had to pack."

"When will you be returning?" Doc asked.

Joe shook his head. "I'm not sure."

Did her shoulders slump slightly at his reply, or had he imagined it?

"Go easy with your back," Doc said, stepping into the aisle.

To his relief, Joe saw that the pastor was engaged in conversation with an elderly woman at the front bench. He was terrified that they might drag him up and introduce him to the preacher, and then everyone might start asking about his salvation. He had been embarrassed like that once when he was seven, and he had never forgotten it.

They moved with the crowd, out of the tent, into the lingering daylight of an August day. He looked up at the sky as he placed his broad-brimmed hat back on his head. Only another hour, two if they were lucky, of daylight. He had to say goodbye and leave.

"Well, thanks again," he said to Ruth, trying to sound more formal with her.

"You're welcome. Take care," she said, extending her hand.

He was surprised by that gesture, surprised even more by the softness of her hand in his, and how much he liked the feel of her slim fingers. Then she had withdrawn her hand and was stepping back from him.

"Good-bye," he said, touching the brim of his hat as he looked from Ruth to Doc Wright. Then he turned and walked toward his horse. It was a sorrel, not particularly handsome, just serviceable, but with a good heart, like his dog Kenai, who waited for him at the boardinghouse.

"Good-bye," her voice called out, but he tried not to hear her.

And all the way back to the boardinghouse, he tried to shut out the murmurings of his conscience and the pain in his heart.

❧

Ruth and her father sat at the kitchen table having a bedtime snack. A patient had been waiting on their doorstep once they arrived back at the clinic. Tom Haroldson, a sixteen-year-old boy, had taken a fall and sprained his ankle while helping his father unload a wagon of supplies. Doc had bound the ankle carefully while Ruth handed him gauze, and now they had closed up the clinic and were free to relax.

"You're a good cook," her father said, taking one last bite of the huckleberry cobbler she had whipped up when they returned from church.

"Thanks."

Ruth had been filled with energy that she needed to vent, and after the clinic, the kitchen was the most appropriate spot to vent her energy, or frustration, whichever it happened to be. She was feeling a bit of both as she toyed with the dessert on her plate and thought about Joe Spencer. She gave up trying to finish the cobbler and laid her fork across the plate.

"Father," she looked up, "when you first met Mother, how did you feel about her?"

His eyes widened at her sudden question, but as usual he took their conversation in stride and always answered her patiently. She was grateful for that.

She watched him thoughtfully as he leaned back in the

chair, and his hazel eyes drifted into space, seeing something that she could not. After a while, he spoke in a soft, gentle voice, one that held the tenderness of a deep love.

"I met her at the home of a friend in Seattle. You've heard the story. But how did I feel?" He heaved a deep sigh. "I thought she had the sweetest spirit of any woman I had ever encountered. I sensed this as we began to talk, and I knew I had never met anyone like her."

He closed his eyes for a moment. When he opened them again, he looked directly at Ruth. "She was pretty, of course, and she could have taken her pick of men." A slow, pleased smile crinkled his face. "Thank God, she chose me."

"I know why," Ruth said softly, placing her elbows on the table, lacing her fingers together to cup her chin. "I would have chosen you if I had been Mother."

Doc's smile widened even more, and for a moment, he said nothing; he merely stared at her. Then he glanced down at the cobbler and took another bite. "Does this question have anything to do with Joe Spencer?" He glanced back at her. "I saw the look in your eyes, Ruth; in fact, I've been watching you all evening."

She reached for her fork, dragging it over the brown crust of the cobbler. "He seems like a nice man, and there aren't many of those around," she said, trying to sound casual.

Doc nodded. "That's true. And he's a gentleman; I like that. But we know very little about him, even though he spent an hour here today, had lunch with us, and joined us at prayer meeting. Still. . ." His voice trailed and now he seemed to be avoiding her eyes.

Ruth didn't like the look of concern on his face or the guarded tone of his voice.

"We haven't had a chance to get to know him," she pointed out. "We've just met him."

"True," he said, lifting his eyes to her face again. "So you must give yourself time to get to know him before you let your heart sweep you away."

"*Fa-ther!*" She lifted an eyebrow and pretended to be dismayed by his words. "Surely you don't think I'm foolish enough to fall for a man I don't know!"

He studied her face for a moment, then the worried lines along his brow softened as the smile touched his face again. "Sorry. A father has to be protective," he said, winking at her.

"Even when his daughter is twenty-one years of age? Please give me credit for not having made a bad choice yet."

They laughed together; but even as she spoke the words, the anxious tone of her voice was apparent to her own ears. She supposed her father heard it as well.

❧

Joe surveyed the area that had been home to Ivan the previous winter. Situated on higher ground, the area was walled in by spruce and birch trees on three sides, with a view of the broad valley below. Salmonberry and huckleberry bushes grew in abundance on the ridges.

Glancing back to the creek below, his eyes moved over the scarred stumps of spruce trees, long since cut down for firewood. There, at the edge of the bank, a spruce stump had been axed clean and carved in the wood in jagged print was the name *Ivan Bertoff.* This marked his claim; and to Joe's utter surprise, nobody had bothered it. It was the habit of most claims to have a description attached to the name, but since Ivan could not write, he had done well to print his name, which was the extent of his education.

Leaning back, swatting at a pestering mosquito, Joe recalled how he had harbored doubts about the stake even being here when Ivan first told him about his claim. But Ivan had told him the truth about everything. He had even described the tiny log hut he had built as a home for the past winter; now Joe would help Ivan expand it into a decent cabin for the two of them.

Joe ran a hand across his forehead as a troublesome thought took root: How badly would he and Ivan get on one another's nerves during the long cold winter that stretched ahead?

With that question in mind, he turned and looked across at Ivan stretched out on the ground, taking a nap. Ivan was a large man, weighing at least two hundred fifty pounds, and he stood six feet, five or maybe six inches. At fifty years of age, only a fringe of black hair rimmed his large shiny head; however, the black hair grew in abundance on his handlebar mustache. He had shed his flannel shirt, and now the stained undershirt strained across his wide chest and protruding stomach above brown corduroy trousers that had seen better days. He snored loudly, oblivious to the occasional mosquito or gnat nipping at his face.

Joe sighed and sat down on a flat rock to assess his situation. He had met Ivan in a saloon in Skagway. Ivan was a loner, friendly to no one; but if not for Joe, he would have bled to death in an alley behind the Last Dollar Saloon. Joe had found him, face down, a deep cut in the center of his back, his pockets emptied. Ivan had come to Skagway for supplies to keep from paying the high prices in Dawson and had nearly paid for it with his life. With assistance, Joe had dragged him to his tent, summoned help, and eventually saved his life. He had hoped, by this act, to make restitution for the life he had taken in Skagway.

Joe swatted at a mosquito and turned his gaze back to the stake, which Ivan swore marked an abundance of gold. Ivan claimed to have found color in the streams, panned it, and followed its source to this property. As for the claim itself, they would build a shaft and work the claim together, splitting the profits. The small amount of money Ivan had after last winter was stolen from him that night in the alley. Joe had won his trust by saving his life, and in return, Ivan was willing to make him a partner in what he was certain was a real bonanza.

After Ivan had produced a tiny piece of gold tucked deep in his boot, Joe had studied it thoughtfully.

"Bite it," Ivan instructed. "Then you know."

Joe looked from Ivan back to the wrinkled piece of metal. He had heard that gold would bend between the teeth if it were real. Amused, he had washed the nugget, placed it between his teeth, and gently bitten down. The nugget bent.

Ivan laughed, pleased to have proven his word. Operating on instinct, Joe had agreed. After all, he needed to stay on the move; and despite his efforts at mining in Skagway, he had lost money. He believed Ivan, for Ivan had no reason to mention the claim if it were not true. He could simply have healed at Joe's tent then said good-bye. Instead, he had wanted to show his gratitude; furthermore, he had noticed that Joe had a little money.

"Ahh. . ." Ivan struggled to a sitting position and looked across at him.

"Have a good nap?" Joe asked with a grin.

Ivan gave a wag of his bald head and turned to stare at their efforts so far. Fortunately, there was still enough timber around for adding on to his cabin. They had spent hours chopping down the spruce trees and cutting the trees into logs for the ends and sides of the cabin. The hut Joe had spotted when they first arrived was developed into a liveable cabin.

"You sleep?" Ivan squinted at him as he lifted a hammy hand to swat at a mosquito.

Joe shook his head. "No, but I'm ready to work again."

Joe drove himself relentlessly and he knew it. The past few

days had been even worse, for in the back of his mind, he kept seeing Ruth Wright's face, and he kept hearing the voice of the pastor at the prayer service.

Sighing, he came to his feet. He could work as hard as Ivan, who was as strong as a moose, and he would. The month of September had come, and the days were already beginning to grow shorter, colder.

In the days that followed, Joe and Ivan worked side by side, from early until late, until exhaustion finally forced them to relinquish the task. They proved to be quite compatible, for neither had much to say, and the comfortable silence that enveloped them eased the strain of working and living together twenty-four hours a day.

Their work was simple yet complex, since they worked with only two sharp axes and two saws. They had no nails or spikes with which to build the cabin. Therefore, they had to notch the logs. Diligently, they worked, flattening three-inch strips across the bottom and top of each spruce log to ensure the fit of the logs when stacked upon one another. They filled the cracks with a thick layer of moss with the hope of shutting out the black flies and mosquitoes that nagged them now and the icy winds and snows that would torment in winter.

When the cabin was finished, Joe suggested they improve upon Ivan's small plank table. They built another one then made long boxes for their sleeping rolls. When Joe finally crawled into the sleeping roll, his back ached almost unbearably, even though he had applied Doc's liniment. Still, he did not think of his back or of his work; instead, his thoughts turned toward Ruth Wright, and the pain seemed to ease as he closed his eyes and the vision of her lovely face filled his memory.

# *four*

"Ruth, I wanted to ask you something." Mrs. Greenwood had caught up as Ruth and Doc were leaving the tent after the Sunday service.

Reminding herself that the sermon had been on loving one's neighbor, Ruth turned sweetly to face Mrs. Greenwood.

"Good morning, Mrs. Greenwood. And how are you today?" Ruth smiled at the plump woman whose black silk dress stretched tautly across the bodice, threatening to pop the buttons.

"I am well, thank you. I want to invite you and your father to join Mr. Greenwood and me for lunch. I'm inviting Dr. Bradley as well," she added, beaming with satisfaction. It amazed Ruth that Mrs. Greenwood seemed to think she was doing everyone a favor with her efforts at matchmaking.

Behind the smile, Ruth gritted her teeth. What was she going to do about Mrs. Greenwood's self-appointed mission to play cupid between Ruth and Dr. Bradley, their competition? Of course, he wasn't really competition, because it took both doctors to tend to the patients in and around Dawson City.

"I. . .think we'll be busy, won't we, Father?" She turned, looking for her father. To her disappointment, he was engaged in conversation with Arthur Bradley.

"I'll just ask," Mrs. Greenwood said. Whirling, she rushed upon the two men, surprising them with the invitation before either could provide an excuse.

Ruth was uncomfortable with the situation. Dr. Bradley had

45

been attempting to court her for the past month, but she had managed to avoid him. He stood about five feet, ten inches, was slight of build, with a long face, thin brown hair, and pale green eyes. He was a pleasant Canadian from Victoria, who had lost his wife to typhoid fever soon after their arrival in Dawson City last July. He had been too grieved to notice anyone until recently, but now she felt his eyes upon her and she didn't know how to respond. She was certain she could never be romantically interested in him.

"We've been invited out for lunch, Ruth," her father called to her, unable to escape the Greenwoods.

"Did you decide not to rest?" Ruth asked, holding her smile in place. "When we left home, you said you needed to get back and lie down, that you're exhausted from the week."

Doc hesitated, obviously caught in the dilemma.

"Then you'll be glad to know the meal is already prepared and waiting on the stove," Mrs. Greenwood shot back at her then turned to Dr. Bradley. "We'll excuse you busy people soon after you eat," she said, fairly beaming at him.

Ruth's eyes lingered on Mrs. Greenwood's round face. Her protruding blue eyes were fixed on Dr. Bradley as though she considered him to be the catch of the century.

Dr. Bradley, obviously embarrassed, nodded and thanked her profusely for her luncheon invitation while casting a quick glance toward Ruth.

Ruth was thoroughly embarrassed by Mrs. Greenwood's obvious attempts to pair up Ruth and the most eligible bachelor in Dawson City. It took every ounce of willpower to hold her temper. She lived up to the reputation of a redhead having a temper, and she was engaged in a mental tug-of-war between minding the pastor's sermon or minding her own will. She could feel the blood rushing to her cheeks. It felt as though her smile had tightened to a grimace of pain. Saying nothing more, she merely looked at her father with an expression that spoke volumes.

"What else could I do?" he muttered under his breath as he tucked her hand in his arm and they made their way to the Greenwood home.

❧

Mrs. Greenwood had seated Ruth opposite Dr. Bradley, with her father at her side, while the Greenwoods occupied opposite ends of the table. Ruth touched the lace tablecloth, appreciating the luxury here in Dawson City. Her eyes moved on to the huge serving platter where a moose roast was surrounded with carrots and potatoes. She was grateful that someone else was willing to go to the trouble of a nice meal for her, and she turned her eyes back to Mrs. Greenwood, determined to be a bit nicer.

"This is very kind of you, Mrs. Greenwood," she said, smiling at the plump woman whose round cheeks were reddened from the heat of the kitchen.

"My pleasure. Mr. Greenwood, will you say grace?"

Everyone bowed their head while thanks were offered for the meal. Then, upon conclusion of the prayer, Ruth unfolded her napkin and laid it across the lap of her gray taffeta dress.

"Dr. Bradley, we've hardly had a chance to talk," Doc said, opening the conversation.

"We stay much too busy, don't we? And I'd like everyone to call me Arthur," he said as his eyes slid to Ruth.

"Arthur," Mrs. Greenwood spoke up, "do you miss Victoria? I hear it's such a beautiful city with the lovely gardens and all."

Sadness gripped his features for a moment as he nodded. "Yes, I do. And I miss Katherine terribly."

"Arthur, may I tell you what helped me when I lost my wife?" Doc asked gently.

The man looked up, his expression bleak. "Please do."

"My pastor recommended that I read the epistles of Paul in the New Testament. Paul was a man who survived shipwrecks, beatings, imprisonment, and starvation. In fact, he suffered numerous adversities and yet he was able to maintain an inner peace throughout his tribulations. Knowing that a man had suffered through so much and kept his faith helped me to hang on to mine. By reading those epistles, I found a peace that I thought was impossible. There isn't a day that passes that I don't long for Mary Ruth, but I have been able to start over and I, too, have found peace."

Arthur stared at Doc for a moment then nodded. "I appreciate your telling me that. Perhaps I will make that effort, as well."

Silence fell, and for a moment even Mrs. Greenwood seemed at a loss for words.

"Which route did you travel getting here?" Doc asked, moving to another subject. "I'm always curious about the various routes people use because it's such a treacherous journey."

"Yes, it is," Arthur agreed. "We took a steamer from Victoria, and actually the trip was quite pleasant. When weather and sea permitted, we stood on deck admiring the scenery. Everything went extremely well until someone on the boat got sick, and then an epidemic of typhoid spread. Fortunately, there was another doctor traveling as far as Lake Bennet. We were able to save some, but we lost many others. We had only been here three days when Katherine came down with typhoid." He dropped his eyes to his lap. "I did not have the facilities or the proper medicine for her. I will regret this trip until my dying day."

Ruth stared at him, moved by his words. She was suddenly filled with compassion for him, and she made a silent vow to be nicer to him. He was not interested in courting her, she decided; he was merely lonely.

Ruth was thinking about what he had said as she looked at him. He seemed so frail for this kind of lifestyle, and she couldn't help wondering why he had wanted to come to this wild frontier. She did not ask him that; instead, she thought of Victoria and how she had always longed to visit the gardens there.

"Do you consider returning to Victoria?" she asked gently.

He nodded. "Yes, I do. I have decided to give myself another year here, and then if I still am not happy, I will return."

Mrs. Greenwood cleared her throat. "Then we must see that you are happy," she said with unnecessary emphasis as she glanced boldly at Ruth. "We need your services here. Dr. Wright can't possibly handle all the people if the exodus continues as they say it will."

"I agree we need his help," Doc said. "However, I think our exodus will soon shut down for the winter. Already the Yukon is starting to freeze over, and Chilkoot and White Pass will be too treacherous in the dead of winter."

"So many people are talking about the scarcity of food." Mr. Greenwood entered the conversation at last. "Nell, do we have enough?"

Everyone stopped chewing and looked at Mrs. Greenwood. "I believe so. What about you people?" She glanced from Doc and Ruth to Arthur.

"I'm afraid I haven't planned very well," Arthur admitted. "Nevertheless, if I continue to be paid in sacks of flour and sugar," a wry grin touched his mouth, "I should fare well."

Doc chuckled. "I imagine we'll soon prefer to be paid in food rather than money."

The rest of the meal passed pleasantly, and after Mrs. Greenwood's bread pudding, Ruth noticed her father had begun to yawn. Everyone had finished the meal and was getting up from the table. She began to help Mrs. Greenwood clear the dishes as the men wandered into the small living room.

"Mrs. Greenwood, exactly when did you come to Dawson?" she asked conversationally, regretting the anger she had felt toward her earlier.

Mrs. Greenwood tilted her head back thoughtfully. "We came in '97, got a head start on getting our cabin built here. Clarence had heard about the strike, of course, and being an assayer, he knew he had a good future here." Her plump face held a wide grin as she spoke.

Ruth nodded. "I'm sure he does." Ruth had heard, through her father, that Mr. Greenwood, as an assayer, was getting rich from collecting remnants of gold dust that gathered on his velvet cloth, not to mention the particles he swept up from the board floor.

"Dear, you must join our sewing circle," Mrs. Greenwood was saying as she scraped the leftover food into a large pail for their dogs.

Ruth had opened her mouth to offer a reply, but she never got the chance. The woman plunged into a discourse on one of the women who was a member of the circle, relating some outrageous gossip.

Ruth glanced toward the living area where the men were seated. She had a chance to look Arthur Bradley over more carefully, since he sat with his back to her. She had to admire the courage required of him to continue on here after losing his wife. He was in a noble profession, like her father, and she admired that, just as she admired the man. Maybe in time she could think of him in a more romantic way. It would certainly make sense for the two of them.

Mrs. Greenwood droned on as Ruth turned back to dry a dish. Suddenly, Ruth's thoughts moved in another direction, and she found herself recalling a handsome bronze face, piercing blue eyes, and golden hair. Joe Spencer. She sighed heavily. It was difficult to believe that she would chose a poor miner over a prosperous doctor whose background seemed more compatible with her own.

Thinking of Joe, she reminded herself that he might not be poor; or if he were low on funds now, he could strike a bonanza like a few men had already done in this area. But then, what did it matter? Money was not the measure of a man.

Her eyes drifted back to the men talking pleasantly in the living room. Even Arthur Bradley was laughing softly. She thought of Joe again, recalling the sheen of tears in his blue eyes. *What had made him sad?* she wondered. And when would she see him again?

She forced her thoughts back to Mrs. Greenwood's prattle, and as they finished in the kitchen, she was relieved to hear her father say he was overdue for his Sunday afternoon nap.

As they prepared to leave, Arthur approached her, looking unsure of himself. "I told your father I'd like to come for a visit sometime to see how his clinic is set up."

She nodded. "Feel free to do that." She realized this was the moment she should have invited him for a meal, but she chose not to do that. Before she could consider Arthur as a suitor, she had to get Joe Spencer out of her head.

≈

One day had begun to flow into another as Joe worked beside Ivan digging through the hard earth, hoping to hit a streak of gold. At night, they built a fire and kept it going. By morning, the fire had served to thaw the ground five to six inches deep so they could start to shovel their way down, making a shaft. They dug fervently until they reached frozen ground again. The following night they built another fire; the next day they dug.

It was a monotonous process of grueling work. Sometimes Joe's back ached so miserably he could hardly sleep. Still, he had spotted some flecks of gold in the black gravel, and now he was filled with hope. This fueled his determination to keep going until they were twenty feet down and four feet wide. This would be their shaft. At this point, they would no longer use a shovel but rather a windlass for getting the dirt out. They took turns in the shaft, shoveling out the rocks and frozen dirt that had melted from the fire. Ivan had made a pigtail hook on the end of the rope attached to the bucket that hauled up the dirt. One man loaded the bucket while the other operated the windlass at the top of the shaft, hauling the bucket to the surface.

Both Ivan and Joe kept their eyes strained for the sight of gold, so much so that they often dreamed about it at night; but through it all, he never stopped thinking of Ruth Wright.

❧

The first snow of the season had come, and Ruth stared out at the swirling snowflakes beyond her window, drawing her shawl tighter around her. She and her father were comfortable and warm in their house, and for that she was grateful. Looking out on the inhabitants of Dawson Creek, huddling into their coats and rushing toward their destination, she wondered just how low the temperature would drop. Already the men wore their fur caps, twill parkas, and heavy mackinaws. Most had shaved their beards. Miners had been warned that in winter their beards would freeze to their face.

The snow did not last, however, and to everyone's surprise the sun burst forth, thawing out the snow, making it possible for the boat that had been docked for a week to depart.

"Ruth," her father entered the room, "check our pantry again."

She turned and glanced at her father as he sank into the

chair, looking weary although it was only ten in the morning. He had already seen three patients, however, and she wondered if he were hungry.

"Do you want an early lunch?" she asked.

He shook his head. "I'm not hungry. I'm just concerned about the food supply. Yesterday, I saw a notice on the board by the trading company that troubled me."

Ruth looked at him curiously. "What is it?"

"Today's boat will probably be the last one until spring. The notice warned those who did not have a supply of food to last the winter to leave Dawson." His hazel eyes were troubled as he looked across at Ruth. "There is a general fear of starvation, so we must be careful."

Ruth nodded then wondered why her father was so generous to his patients if he had concerns about their food. She had watched thin men and women haul tinned goods from their clinic by the armload. Still, she was not worried. She knew her father was doing the Christian thing by giving hungry people food.

She had examined their pantry just this morning as she was planning the day's meals. The shelves were still fully stocked, although there were some obvious spaces where tinned goods had once been, the results of her father's generosity. It didn't matter. She would be a smart cook, and her father had a promise from one of the merchants that there was a supply of food tucked in a back room for the doctors and merchants.

She smiled at him, aware that he needed her reassurance. "We will be fine, Father. There's plenty of food in our pantry, and I have learned how to economize."

He sighed with relief. "I'm glad to hear that." He ran a hand across his forehead. "Ruth, I think I'll lie down for a few minutes. Keep an eye on the clinic, please."

"Of course," she said. Her eyes followed him with concern.

He seemed to be moving slowly today, and she knew he worried too much about her and about his patients.

After he had gone to his room, she went to the kitchen to stir the hash simmering in the iron skillet. She loved the smell of onions and potatoes that filled her kitchen. Since this was one of her father's favorite meals, perhaps it would boost his energy.

She went to the window and glanced out. There was no one approaching their door. Still, she should go downstairs and wait in the clinic while her father rested. They kept medicine in the supply cabinet and her father worried about theft.

Halfway down the stairs, she thought she heard her father call her name. She hesitated, her hand on the banister. Then she heard the unmistakable sound of a loud groan. Lifting her skirts, she flew back up the stairs.

"Father?" she called out as she entered the quiet living room. Hurrying on to his bedroom, her eyes flew to his bed and her breath caught. "*Father!*"

His legs were extended from the bed onto the floor, while his upper torso remained slumped against the bed. It looked as though he had made an attempt to get up then given up.

"Father? What is it?" She rushed to the bed.

When she looked into his face, fear slammed into her. His eyes were open, staring at the ceiling. For a split second she froze, unable to move. She had watched men die in her role as nurse, but she refused to believe what her knowledge suggested to her now. Seizing his limp hand, she began to rub it earnestly, calling his name all the while. He did not respond, did not move. And now his eyes were glazed. She put a hand to his neck, seeking the pulse point, finding none.

A cry escaped her as she flew into the living room, grabbing her cloak from its hook. Down the stairs and out the door she went, not bothering to lock the door, disobeying her father's cardinal rule. All she could think of was reaching Arthur Bradley's office two blocks down the street.

The people she passed along the way were a blur; someone called to her. She ran wildly, oblivious to the cold penetrating her dress and shawl, to the harsh wind biting her face. She was too numb with fear to feel anything other than the need to get help.

Her breath jerked in her throat, sending gasps of cold air down to pierce her lungs. She burst into the door marked Dr. Bradley and found him examining a patient. At her abrupt entrance, Arthur Bradley removed the stethoscope from the man's chest and stared at her.

"What is it?" he asked, taking in her windblown hair, her white face.

"Father!" Her voice was a whimper, but he understood and grabbed his coat.

"What about me, Doctor?" The patient called after him.

Ignoring him, Arthur grabbed his black bag and ran out the door with Ruth. She tried to explain what had happened as they ran the distance, but her voice was breaking in sobs.

"Don't try to talk," Arthur said as they raced along the boardwalks, attracting stares as they hurried up the hill to Ruth's house.

Her legs were weakening, more from her emotion than exhaustion. Arthur glanced at her. "Slow down. I'll get there as quickly as I can."

She lagged back, her chest aching from the hard run, her cheeks oddly cold. She pressed her fingers against her cheeks and felt the moisture. She blinked, aware for the first time that she was crying, and now the cold air struck her wet cheeks, chilling her more. In the distance, she could hear the boat's whistle, signaling its departure; and she recalled her father's last warning about this being the last day to leave town.

*What's wrong with me?* she thought wildly. *Why have I stopped thinking of Father's condition? Of Arthur racing on ahead? Why am I standing on the boardwalk staring back at the boat dock?*

Someone touched her arm. She whirled. It was Mrs. Greenwood. "Dear, is something wrong? You're obviously upset, and you're out without your coat."

Ruth swallowed, giving way to the sobs that wracked her body. "It's Father," she said. "I must get home."

Breaking free of Mrs. Greenwood, she took a breath and forced herself to hurry on. A second burst of energy propelled her, and she tried to think about what must be done. Her father had gone into a coma for some reason; that was it. Dr. Bradley—Arthur—would know what to do. He would give him some kind of medicine, an injection; he would do something to save the man who was the center of her world. And she would be eternally grateful to Arthur. She would accept his invitations, even try to return his interest if only he would save her father.

Those were the thoughts flying through her brain as she reached the house, climbed to the front porch on shaky knees, then stumbled through the front door.

The house was quiet, quieter than she had ever heard it. A different kind of quiet.

Then Arthur was coming down the stairs, his black bag in his hand. Her eyes dropped to the bag then returned to his face. She saw it then, the look of pity, of. . .sympathy.

"No," she said, sinking into the nearest chair. "He's going to be all right." Her words were muffled behind her palms as she cupped her face in her hands, giving way to sobs again. "It can't be," she cried. But she had known the truth before she left the house, and now Arthur confirmed her worst fears.

"I'm sorry." His voice sounded distant in her ringing ears.

"It appears to have been a heart attack. He's. . .gone."

"Please, God. . . ," she pleaded, burying her face deeper in her hands, unwilling to accept it, unwilling to believe it. She had already given up her mother, wasn't that enough? Why her father? Why *now?* He was too young. "No," she said brokenly, shaking her head wildly. She felt an arm around her shoulder, and she heard his voice again.

"I'm so sorry."

The door was opening, and she could hear Mrs. Greenwood's voice, but she refused to look at her or to listen to Arthur.

"I'm going to give you an injection, Ruth." His voice was weaker now as another arm embraced her, a heavier arm. "You're going into shock." The words made no sense to her, just as nothing else did.

Her sleeve was being pushed up, and the woman beside her was speaking gently. Something pricked her arm, but she scarcely felt it. The woman continued to talk, and the man said something as well, but it didn't matter. Nothing mattered. She slumped against the arms that held her as her senses hurried toward the comforting darkness that enveloped her.

## *five*

Joe and Ivan were getting low on food and supplies, and both were in need of a new pair of rubber overshoes. Long since out of kerosene for their lantern, they had to dig by candlelight. Joe jumped at the excuse to go into Dawson, for it had been two months since he had been to town. Ivan, preferring solitude, was happy to leave this task to Joe.

Bundled into a heavy parka, Joe spent an extra minute petting Kenai, who seemed to be taking the cold well, and promised him a thick bone on his return.

Eight hours later, his felt hat lowered on his forehead to protect him against the wind and huddled into his parka, he rode into Dawson.

The little town of Dawson was a welcome sight to him after weeks out in the bush. He turned his horse in at the hitching rail before Miss Mattie's Roadhouse. As he swung down from the horse, a blast of wind whipped across his face, and he quickened his steps, hoping there was a spare cot.

To his good fortune, there was one cot left, and a pot of hot coffee waited on the stove for those coming in from the cold.

"Warm yourself," Miss Mattie said, motioning him onto a bench at the long wooden table.

She was a stout woman who usually dressed in her husband's trousers and flannel shirts and wore her hair slicked back in a bun. Her lack of femininity in appearance was compensated for in her tasty food and clean, comfortable home.

"Thank you," Joe said, easing down onto the bench and

sipping at the coffee. "Mighty good," he said, giving her his best smile.

She hesitated for a moment, staring into his face. Then she glanced back at the stove. "Got some dumplings on the stove if you're hungry."

Joe hesitated, not wanting to impose, and yet he hadn't eaten since last night. He recalled his meal of cold beans and hard tack and his stomach growled.

Miss Mattie, unaccustomed to being argued with, was already dipping out some dumplings in a small tin pan.

"Better stock up with groceries before you head back," she said, placing the pan down before him. "No more boats are coming in till spring, and the stores are already starting to ration food. It will get scarce. Did last winter."

He nodded; then as he tasted the dumplings, he realized that renting a cot did not cover good food as well. "Miss Mattie, I don't feel right eating your food unless you add a little more to my bill. Please do that."

Her gray eyes shot to him, then she shrugged. "All right. Another dollar will cover you. How long did you say you'll be staying here?"

Joe was enjoying the taste of the rich dumplings so much that it took a moment for him to swallow and reply. "Just long enough to pick up some supplies." Then his thoughts moved on to one of his reasons for returning to Dawson. Ruth Wright. "I may need to stop in at Doc Wright's clinic and get him to check my back again."

She whirled from the stove and looked at him with an expression of surprise. "Haven't you—no, you've been out in the bush," she said, answering her own question. "Guess you can't keep up with the town news. Doc Wright died almost two months ago. Heart attack."

Joe almost dropped his fork. He stared at Miss Mattie for a

moment. "What about. . .what will happen to his clinic?"

Miss Mattie sighed and shrugged. "It's closed down. There's only one doctor left, Arthur Bradley, and he's still wet behind the ears. I shouldn't say that. Most folks think he's all right. He just suffers in comparison to Doc Wright." Her chest heaved beneath the flannel shirt. "It's a tragedy for Dawson City that we've lost Doc."

Joe stared into space, shaking his head. "He was a nice man. I liked him a lot." He cleared his throat. "What about his daughter? Is she still here?"

"The last boat had pulled out the day he died." She shook her head. "It's a shame she couldn't go back to Seattle. I heard she was all tore up about Doc's death." She was pouring flour into a large bowl. Then she added two handfuls of sugar. "She's a good nurse, though. I hear she wouldn't see anybody for a while, then Dr. Bradley persuaded her to go to work for him in his clinic. Nell Greenwood says they'll probably team up. Nell's the town crier, you know."

Joe arched an eyebrow. "No, I don't know her."

"Then you've missed being grilled about where you come from and what you're doing here."

"Is that right?" He made a mental note to avoid the woman at all costs.

"Yep. Nell keeps up with everybody's business."

"What do you mean about Miss Wright and Dr. Bradley teaming up?" Joe frowned, hoping this meant they would team up as the local nurse and doctor.

Miss Mattie turned back to the stove. "Dr. Bradley and Ruth Wright are sharing Thanksgiving dinner with the Greenwoods. Nell says there's a romance in the making. Dr. Bradley's a widower, you know?" she asked, glancing back over her shoulder.

Joe stared into his plate. "No, I don't know him." Nor did

he want to know him if Ruth was interested in him. "Where does he come from?" he couldn't resist asking.

"Victoria. He's a nice man, little too nice for Dawson, if you ask me."

Joe nodded. He could see how Ruth would have a lot in common with someone like that, and if she worked in his clinic, perhaps it would help her to survive a long, cruel winter.

"Don't you like my dumplings?" Miss Mattie asked, thrusting her hands on her hips and staring at his half-filled plate.

"They're wonderful. I think my stomach just shrunk a bit since I've been doing my own cooking."

He picked up the fork and tried to resume his meal with enthusiasm, but he was merely going through the motions in order not to offend Miss Mattie. His thoughts were centered on Ruth, and he found himself filled with a mix of emotions. He had been unable to get her out of his mind since leaving Dawson City. In fact, his plan had been to clean up a bit then head right over to the clinic. Miss Mattie's bad news had changed everything.

He stared at the scarred plank boards of the eating table. Doc Wright had been a good, decent man. Joe was saddened by the news of his death. He was glad he had attended church with them, and yet he had sensed a cautiousness about the man where his daughter was concerned. Joe could certainly understand why. Doc had gone out of his way to be kind to him, and yet Joe had watched a wall of reserve going up when he caught Joe staring at Ruth.

Thinking back, he recalled that it had been Ruth who invited him to church, and she had smiled at him as though she liked him. Doc had noticed that, of course.

Joe sighed, pushing his plate aside. In comparison with this city-bred doctor, he had nothing to offer. No matter how much he wanted to see Ruth Wright, he must force himself to stay away from her now. She would be much better off with Bradley.

He came slowly to his feet, feeling tired to the bone. "You asked how long I'll be here. I'll only be staying the night. As soon as I round up what I need, I'll be riding out in the morning."

Miss Mattie nodded. "Then I'll have you some hot biscuits on the stove."

"Thanks," he said, trying to smile.

His heart was not in his smile nor his words. He felt a keen disappointment welling up inside. He should be accustomed to the feeling by now, but he was not. Particularly not where Ruth Wright was concerned. Being in her presence had awakened something deep in his soul. It was as though a candle had been lit in the darkness. He had been happy. But now the candle had been extinguished.

ða

Ruth stood in the Dawson City cemetery staring bleakly at her father's grave. A cold wind raced across the frozen Yukon and snatched at the hood of her black woolen cloak. The hood gave way and now her auburn hair was exposed to the elements, but she didn't care. Nor did she care that she had lost weight and looked as devastated as she felt.

As she stared at the mound of dirt that covered her father, thick tears streamed down her cold cheeks. Absently, she thrust her kid glove into the deep pocket of her skirt and withdrew the crumpled lace handkerchief he had given her, one of many Christmas gifts last year.

She touched the soft handkerchief to her eyes, then her nose, and sniffed hard.

"Good-bye for today, Father," she spoke softly. "I know you and Mother are together. . .safe and happy. . .together in heaven."

While that knowledge brought her comfort, at the same time she was filled with the deepest sense of loneliness and despair that she had ever known. She was completely alone here in this frozen country, cut off from the world until late next spring or whenever the weather warmed enough to thaw the Yukon River. Alone except for Arthur, who had been so very kind to her.

She took a deep quivering breath, refusing to allow pity or regret to get a foothold in her heart. She was glad she had come here with her father; she would feel worse if she had thwarted his last dream.

She pulled her hood over her head and turned from the grave. Squaring her shoulders, she drew her slender body erect, trying to call forth the strength she knew she would need to survive. As she walked back toward home, she paid little attention to the people hurrying in and out of shops or the occasional miner and his mule or his dogs. She thought of stopping in to see Arthur on this Sunday. It would be nice to visit on a day when the clinic was closed. But she wasn't even up to attending church services this morning, and now she didn't feel like a social call. All she wanted was to lock herself in her house, curl up in bed, and sleep. Arthur told her that wasn't healthy, that she must go on with her life. It was exactly what her father would say. In fact, her father had liked Arthur and would be pleased to know that he was calling on her.

She sighed. In time, God would restore her if she clung to His promises and kept reading her mother's Bible. It was all that gave her comfort and hope now. As she reached her house, she quickened her pace, climbing the steps and unlocking the door.

She was going to put the teakettle on and make a pot of tea. She was trying to drink more tea and less coffee, since coffee was being rationed at the mercantile. She still had a good supply in the pantry, but she knew she must be saving with it.

As always, the echo of her footsteps on the boards in the hall reminded her of how quiet the house was and how alone she felt. Arthur had offered to buy the house, but she didn't know where that would leave her, and she wasn't ready to think about a permanent relationship with him. Not yet. Perhaps in time.

⁂

Joe strapped his newly purchased supplies onto the horse and glanced up at the sky. He had been pleased to see sunshine when he awoke and peered through the window by his cot. When he entered Miss Mattie's kitchen, she had informed him that it was going to be a pleasant day. Her hot coffee and thick biscuits had reinforced her prediction.

He placed his boot into the stirrup and pulled himself into the saddle. Turning the horse's head, he trotted through town, trying to forget that he must pass the clinic in the next block. Miss Mattie's words had stayed with him throughout the night. It should have been his best night's sleep in weeks, but he had slept fitfully. The room was warm, the cot was comfortable, and the men occupying other cots had not snored loudly enough to bother him. Ruth Wright bothered him. What would happen to her?

It was not his business, he told himself as he approached her frame house, yet he couldn't resist a quick glance in that direction. The house looked forlorn, with the curtains drawn and no one coming or going. His eyes strayed to the front door, and he thought about how welcome he had felt when he walked through that door and how good the Wrights had been to him. He continued to stare at the house, hoping that a curtain would part, that he would see her face framed in the window. Then he would feel he had an excuse to stop by and say hello. But the curtains remained closed and the door did not open.

He turned his eyes back to the road before him. Soon he would be out of Dawson City, heading back to the crude cabin he shared with Ivan for the winter. That knowledge brought a weight to his heart, and for a moment he could hardly resist the temptation to go back to the Wright house to speak with Ruth.

No, he had made himself a promise not to interfere in her life now. He drew a deep breath and forced his eyes toward the other travelers along the road. Occasionally, he met another miner coming or going, their faces haggard, their eyes weary.

The craze for gold—it gripped all of them and held them tight. It kept them digging into the frozen ground, hauling up bucket after bucket of dirt, searching, hoping, praying for the sight of gold flecks, nuggets, or yes—a vein of gold that would transport them from rags to riches.

Glancing at the last tent on the edge of town, his eyes froze. It was the tent that served as a church, the church he had attended with the Wrights. The tent was emptying of people, and he realized this was Sunday and the service had just concluded.

He pulled on the reins to halt his sorrel and sat back in the saddle, staring at the people coming out of the tent. Ruth was not among them. Had she stopped going to church? He frowned. That possibility troubled him; it would mean she was as distraught as Miss Mattie had indicated.

His eyes lifted to the snow-covered roof of the tent. Ruth and her father had brought him here, opened a door in his heart that he thought he had firmly closed. Still, that door they had opened was ajar, and he had been nagged by a longing to return to God. Once upon a time there had been peace in his life, peace when he had lived by God's rules. But for a long time he had lived by his own rules.

It took several seconds for him to realize that he and his horse had come to a dead halt in the center of the road, that he was simply staring at the strangers who must think his behavior odd.

He turned his eyes to the road ahead, but something more important lingered in his mind. Doc Wright and his daughter had brought something good back into his life, if only for a short while. He had found peace inside that tent during their little church service. He wasn't back on the spiritual path yet, but he felt the call, as surely as he felt the call to search for Klondike gold.

He shifted in his saddle and glanced back over his shoulder. The very least he could do was express his sympathy to her and his thanks for what she and her father had done for him. There was something wrong about riding into town and then leaving without at least paying his respects.

Gently, he turned the horse's head and trotted back toward Ruth Wright's house.

# six

Ruth stood at the stove, stirring the stew. She had decided to make use of some remnants in the pantry, making an odd mix of what she could find. She cooked conservatively these days, but she had no appetite, and even if she did, she knew she had to be careful with her food supply.

She heard the whinny of a horse and removed her wooden spoon and laid it on the spoon rest. Wearily, she walked to the window to look down, wondering which patient had not heard about her father's death. She had turned so many away, although on three occasions she had been able to help. She had served as midwife for two babies and bandaged up one minor cut.

When her glance fell on Joe Spencer getting down from his horse, her breath caught. For a moment she stood mesmerized, watching him slowly loop the reins of his horse around the log hitching rail. Then suddenly she came alive. Her hands flew to her hair, patting it back into the chignon as she turned and hurried down the steps to the front door, just as he began to knock.

Of course she had thought of him many times the past weeks, wondered about him. Still, she had resigned herself to the fact that it would be a long time before she saw him again, if ever. Like so many others, she thought he might have given up and left Dawson.

Turning the key in the lock, she opened the door and looked into his serious blue eyes. For the first time in days, she felt a little smile creep over her mouth.

"Hello," she said as he removed his hat. "Come in."

He hesitated for a moment, scraping the soles of his boots on the mat. She found herself thinking of the many others who never bothered to do that.

She held the door back for him as he stepped inside the hall, and she stepped back from him then closed the door. The cold air whipped in with him, bringing a smell of spruce and horseflesh and a pleasant soap. He was wearing a heavy parka over jeans and chaps; his boots were clean.

He was staring at the closed door of the clinic. She wondered for a moment if he knew, but the sadness in his eyes told her that he did.

"Would you like a cup of tea?" she asked.

He looked back at her, his hat pressed against his chest. "Thank you. I'd like that very much."

She nodded. "Come on up."

He paused long enough to hook his hat and coat on the hall tree, then he followed her up the stairs.

Lifting her skirts to climb the stairs, she wondered fleetingly if this was proper, having Joe Spencer up to her kitchen when they were alone in the house. Proper no longer mattered in this situation. She was glad to see this man, and she wanted to know what he had been doing since she last saw him.

As they entered the living room, the warmth from the cook stove reached them. She glanced over her shoulder. "I don't heat the downstairs now."

He nodded. "Good idea. Miss Wright. . . ," he began then faltered.

She knew what he was trying to say and tried to smile. "I'm glad you stopped by," she answered, turning toward the kitchen. "Did you just arrive?"

His boots echoed over the wooden boards as he entered the kitchen. "No. I came last night. I needed supplies."

She was pouring tea into the cup, and now she glanced over the curl of steam as she handed the cup to him. "I see," she said, registering the fact that he hadn't rushed right over as she had dared to hope.

He cleared his throat as she poured herself a cup of tea and motioned him toward the kitchen table.

"Actually, I had planned to stop in when I arrived late yesterday," he was saying as he settled into a chair opposite her at the table. "Then I heard the bad news about your father. . ."

She dropped her eyes, staring into the dark tea.

"I wanted to come and tell you how sorry I am," he said in a gentle voice. "You must be completely grief stricken."

She nodded, averting her eyes. "I am." She swallowed hard. Surely there were no tears left, but she could feel her throat tighten in a threat. "I've had an awful time adjusting. In fact, for the first two weeks, I couldn't even leave the house. I just sat here and cried." She took a deep breath and then looked at him. "I've gone to work at Dr. Bradley's clinic and that seems to help. At least, it keeps my mind off my own situation."

"What are your plans?"

She sighed. "My plans? I'm afraid I don't have any plans." She lifted her eyes and looked around the kitchen. "I've sold most of the medical supplies to Dr. Bradley." She wondered why he suddenly dropped his eyes to the tea, not looking at her. "I've kept a few necessary items—gauze, first aid supplies, that sort of thing. Is there anything you might like to take back to camp?" she asked suddenly.

He looked up, appearing surprised by the question. "I. . . don't think so."

"How is your back?" she asked, sipping her tea for the first time.

He shrugged. "It still aches when I abuse it." He grinned.

"But the liniment helped a lot."

"Good." Her eyes locked with his for a moment as silence fell. Then she remembered her stew. "I was about to have an early lunch. Could I offer you a bowl of stew?"

He hesitated, glanced at the stove, then shook his head. "I had breakfast at Miss Mattie's."

"Then my cooking can't compare to hers, I'm afraid."

"Sure it does," he answered quickly, too quickly, and they both smiled. "I just don't want to impose," he added softly, smiling at her.

She shook her head. "You aren't. To be honest, I get tired of eating alone."

"Oh." She saw the question in his eyes, but then he glanced toward the pot of stew. "In that case, I would be honored to join you." He placed his teacup on the table. "May I wash up?"

She indicated the pan of water on the basin. "Sure."

Ruth stood and began to assemble the bowls and spoons, feeling something awaken in her heart again. She had felt completely numb ever since she walked into the room and found her father on the bed, breathing his last breath. In fact, she had begun to wonder if her heart, like the frozen ground, would ever thaw again. Now, as she busily dipped the stew into bowls and heard his movements in the background, she felt the cold begin to break inside her. She felt a nudge of warmth, a ray of hope.

When they sat down at the table, she offered grace. Then, as she unfolded her napkin and glanced at him, she found herself recalling the prayer service, the look in his eyes when the service ended. She knew he had been touched, and now she felt as though she should return to that moment. Perhaps that was the reason God had placed him in her life.

"When are you leaving?" she asked, already hating the thought.

"Today," he responded, looking across at her. "I wish I could stay longer. In fact," he lowered his eyes to his spoon as he dipped into the stew, "if I had known about. . ." He looked up at her. "I would have come into Dawson for your father's funeral if I had known."

"Thank you," she said, touched by his kindness. "Pastor Sprayberry conducted a graveside service reading Father's favorite verses. After Mother's death, Father told me not to be sad for him when his time came. He thought the end of one's life should be a celebration—"

"A celebration?" Joe Spencer was obviously taken aback.

"Yes, he believed that we should be thankful for a person's life, then celebrate his passing to a better world."

He chewed for a moment, staring at her, obviously thinking about what she had said. "That makes a lot of sense. It's too bad more people don't have that kind of attitude."

She lifted a shoulder in a weak shrug. "Well, of course there's the grief in a loved one's passing. . .but I know he's with Mother." She looked at Joe and this time there was no stopping the tears that formed in her eyes. "They were so devoted to one another. They must be very happy to be reunited."

His eyes widened as he put down his soup spoon and tilted his head, studying her thoughtfully. "That must be very comforting to you."

"Yes, it's comforting," she agreed, "but it's a truth that I feel very deeply. I know they're together in heaven."

He dropped his eyes to his napkin, saying nothing in response.

She leaned forward in her chair, curious to know his thoughts. "How do you feel about those things? Or is that too personal?"

When he looked back at her, a gentle smile crossed his lips, lighting his blue eyes. "You've been very open with me. It would be selfish on my part not to share my thoughts with you."

She blinked, surprised by his statement. She was just beginning to realize what a tender, caring person he was. She was hungry to know more about him, to know everything.

"I don't usually talk about this," he said, "but somehow I feel comfortable talking with you. I've already told you my father died soon after he returned from war, that I was a baby."

"Yes, I've thought of what you said about reading his diary. I think that must have been so special."

He nodded. "It was. But then when my mother died. . ." He broke off, frowning.

She studied the way the skin between his brows puckered with the frown, and she saw the blue eyes dim with the memory. She could feel his sadness, as real as her own, and at that moment, she knew they shared a bond that was special.

"What happened when your mother died?" she prompted.

"I suppose each of us reacted differently. My older brothers seemed to go on with their lives, even though they missed her as I did. But somehow. . ." He shook his head. "I don't know, somehow my life just wasn't the same anymore. I grew restless, tired of Richmond. I wasn't willing to work as a clerk in a store as my brothers were doing. You see, we lost everything in the war. Our plantation was confiscated by the government, all our horses and cattle. Mother took in work as a seamstress soon after I was born. Her father supported us as best he could, but we struggled. Always. I wanted to make a different life for myself. I didn't want to struggle the way others did."

He drained his teacup and Ruth got up to refill it.

"Thank you." He smiled at her.

"I had an uncle who had gone out west right after the war,"

he continued. "Over the years, his letters fired my imagination. I left the South and I can't say that I've really missed it."

She nodded. "So how long did you work in California?"

He picked up the cup and sipped his tea. "I worked my way from Virginia to California," he answered with a smile. "That took a while. Then soon after I got to the ranch where my uncle worked, he died."

"Really?" She sighed. "Your life has been pretty difficult, hasn't it?"

He shrugged. "I don't mean to sound tragic. I never knew my uncle, really. What about you? Did you leave family in Seattle?"

She blinked, trying to follow the quick change of thoughts. "Just an uncle and aunt, and half a dozen cousins."

"Do you plan to return?" he asked, watching her closely.

She nodded. "Probably. I'm not certain I'll go back to Seattle, however." Like Joe, she wasn't ready to face the memories that would accompany her when she went to the large lonely house they had left behind. She had written to ask her uncle to look into selling it. She knew she was going to need the funds.

"I see," he said, pushing his bowl back.

She heard the note of reserve in his tone and wondered what had brought about his change of mood. The fact that she would probably return to the States?

"What are *your* plans?" she asked quickly.

He leaned back in the chair and looked at her, saying nothing for a moment. "My plans are to work my claim for as long as it takes. I believe the gold is there," he said. "And I'm determined not to stop digging until I find it."

His words saddened Ruth, for now she saw in his face the same kind of fierce emotion that seemed to drive so many people here in Dawson, even the merchants.

"Ah, you want to be rich like everyone else who has come here?" she asked.

His expression changed, and she sounded more harsh than she had intended. Still, she had spoken her thoughts honestly.

"Why else would anyone come here?" he asked, an edge to his tone.

She studied him for a moment, wondering if he thought that was the only reason she and her father had come. She was about to set him straight when he suddenly came to his feet.

"I appreciate your hospitality. The stew was delicious. And I enjoyed the company," he said. This time, however, his smile was more reserved.

"Thank you," she said, standing. "And thank you for stopping by."

Silence stretched between them, and for a moment, she thought he might say something. The moment passed, however, as he turned for the door. "Take care of yourself," he said, glancing back over his shoulder.

"You, too," she said, clasping her fingers before her as she followed him through the living room and down the front steps. She watched as he retrieved his coat and hat from the hall tree. "What kind of living conditions do you have at the mine site?" she asked curiously.

"A very small, rather crude cabin," he drawled, buttoning his coat. "I imagine it will shrink even more as the winter progresses. I share it with Ivan," he added, planting his hat firmly on his head and looking her over once more.

"Well. . ." She crossed her arms, wondering what was left to say. "Good luck."

"Thank you."

She watched his expression change once again. The reserve seemed to be slipping, and now his eyes held an emptiness as he glanced at her one last time.

"Good-bye," he finally said, his voice gentle and soft.

"Good-bye," she replied, staring after him as he turned and walked out the door.

For a long time, she stood in the door, oblivious to the cold, watching as he mounted the horse and rode off. Then something her father had said returned to haunt her. *We don't really know him, Ruth.*

She realized how true that was. Each time she felt as though she was on the brink of knowing him well, perhaps on a deeper level than most other people, something happened. She was unsure if she said something that stopped his flow of words, or if he had the ability to shut out painful memories, to stop himself just short of letting anyone see his soul.

When he was out of sight, she closed the door and locked it. Then she pressed her back to the door and stared into space. Her feelings for him were as strong as before, but this time she sensed something more: He was a very complicated man. There were layers to this man that would have to be uncovered before she could allow herself to really care for him.

Shivering, she headed back up the stairs thinking how uncomplicated Arthur Bradley was in comparison. While their conversations were never very exciting, and certainly she did not feel physically attracted to him as she did with Joe, there was something very comforting about being with Arthur. Was it because of his medical background? Was the comfort she found with him due to the familiarity of being in a clinic, hearing the talk she had heard all of her life? Or was it because she knew he cared for her, and she found security in knowing that?

She sighed as she reached the kitchen and stared at Joe's empty bowl and cup. He was, after all, just another money-hungry miner. He had no real mission in life, as she and her father had or even as Arthur had. While Arthur had never gotten around to reading the Bible, as her father had suggested, he was a good man.

She picked up Joe's dishes and took them to the basin, forcing herself to wash them quickly this time, rather than hold the cup as a silly souvenir like she had done before. Joe's visit had served to frustrate and confuse her in one way; in another way, the mystique surrounding him seemed to underscore the logic of returning Arthur's affections.

&

Joe rode back to camp, regretting his visit to Ruth. He was glad he'd had the good manners to pay his respects, but he should have left it at that. He should never have stayed for lunch and an hour of conversation. The lady at the boardinghouse had been right. She did have plans with Bradley; otherwise, why was she hedging about returning to Seattle? *Probably waiting on a marriage proposal,* he told himself bitterly.

He tried to tell himself other things as well: that she was merely pretending that she and her father hadn't been drawn here by the money they would make, that she had regarded him with a certain disdain when he was honest about his reason for being here. He bunched his shoulders together, tugged his hat lower on his forehead as a blast of cold wind hit him. While sitting in the cozy kitchen with her, a wonderful contentment had settled over him. He had felt a sense of home, of caring for someone again. Yes, for an hour, he had felt a frightening pull toward Ruth Wright. He had even been on the brink of telling her many things about himself. He was grateful he had come to his senses in the nick of time. Confiding in her would have been a mistake.

He was not interested in her, he told himself. She was less appealing since she had lost weight. Still, she rode with him, in his thoughts, in his memory; and she was to remain there until he saw her again.

Ruth had accepted the Greenwoods' invitation to join them for Thanksgiving dinner, although the food was less abundant this time, and everyone knew why. The main topic of conversation in Dawson was the fear of running out of food before a boat could bring in more supplies in the spring. Nevertheless, the Greenwoods managed a nice meal, and she had been grateful. She had brought along a loaf of bread and a rice pudding, which Arthur complimented profusely.

"Didn't I see that blond stranger enter your house this week?" Mrs. Greenwood asked bluntly, startling all of them.

Ruth chewed her food, taking her time in replying. "Yes, he stopped in to pay his respects," she answered coolly.

"Well, it might pay to be leery of him," Mr. Greenwood spoke up. "There's something funny going on with that claim."

Ruth looked up quickly. "Why do you say that?"

"The claim belongs to someone else."

Ruth looked at him, wondering why he had spoken in a sinister tone, as though there was something suspicious about Joe. "He has a partner. I'm sure the claim is filed under that man's name," she said, sounding more defensive than she intended. She realized that all three were staring at her, and she guessed they wondered how she happened to know. "He mentioned having a partner to my father and me on the first day he came to the clinic," she added slowly, "with an injured back."

*There, that should shut them up,* she thought, glancing down the table to Mr. Greenwood who was as thin and gaunt as his wife was plump.

"Well, I just wondered," said Mr. Greenwood with a light shrug.

"Ruth," Arthur picked up the conversation tactfully, "we'll

probably be seeing a number of patients tomorrow who have overindulged in Thanksgiving dinners."

She smiled at him, grateful for the kind way he seemed to understand when she needed a change of subject.

"What with the shortage of food, you may not have many patients," Mrs. Greenwood added, coming in from the kitchen with a platter of jam cake.

Ruth smiled then, for she had not had jam cake since she left Seattle, and she was grateful for the Greenwoods' kindness. The least she could do was overlook their tendency to mind other people's business. They were probably unaware of how prevalent their habit was. The day passed pleasantly then, and Arthur even offered to accompany her to the cemetery, where she paid her respects to her father and tried not to cry over the Thanksgivings past. When he walked her home, he seemed to sense her need to be alone then, and he did not linger for an invitation to come inside.

"I'll see you tomorrow," he said at the door.

She nodded. "Arthur, thank you for being so kind."

He smiled at her with tenderness filling his green eyes. "It's easy to be kind to you, Ruth. I long to help you in any way I can."

"I know that," she answered quickly. "Thank you."

After she had gone inside and locked the door, she felt a lingering worry over what to do about Arthur. She could see that he was growing very fond of her, and she wasn't sure how she felt about him. As she had said, she was grateful for his kindness, and she appreciated all he was doing for her. Unfortunately, she could not dredge up any romantic notions toward him. Nor did she imagine that she ever would. Still, she had to be realistic, she told herself, lifting her skirts to climb the stairs. Eager to get her corset off, for she was unaccustomed to wearing one these days, she told herself

that her father would be pleased that she was seeing Arthur
and working in the clinic with him.

On the other hand, she just could not visualize a future with
him, even though it might be the most sensible thing she
could do. Perhaps she was a foolish romantic. . .or perhaps
she would have been better off if she had never met Joe
Spencer.

æ

As winter set in across Dawson, Ruth spent more time helping Arthur in the clinic. Colds, pneumonia, and influenza
were common, and then an outbreak of measles brought on
another swell of patients. Ruth walked home in late afternoon
exhausted, and as she looked around the town, she saw the
sad effects of people struggling to stay warm and fed. Prices
had begun to soar, from lots for building sites to groceries and
hardware. The supplies on board the last boat were drastically
short of food and heavy in liquor, which added to the prob-
lems of the town. More fights broke out in the saloons, more
crime was present. She no longer ventured out beyond the
hours of daylight.

"Ruth, I want to speak seriously to you." Arthur had
detained her one evening in December as she tugged on her
warm gloves and tightened the chin strings of her cloak.

"What is it?" she asked, studying his somber expression.

"I'm very concerned for your welfare," he said, his green
eyes mirroring his concern.

"I feel responsible for you, Ruth. And I know your father
would have wanted me to take care of you. In view of that—"

"Arthur," Ruth put up a hand, "I'm perfectly capable of
taking care of myself. You needn't trouble yourself. You have
enough to worry about with all the patients you're seeing
now."

Arthur shoved his hands into his pants pockets and studied

the thin rag rug. "I'm not saying this well. I didn't mean to imply that you aren't capable. You're the most responsible woman I've ever known." Slowly, his eyes rose to meet hers. "Perhaps I have the cart before the horse, so to speak. I'm the one who needs you."

Ruth paused at the door, her hand on the knob. She turned and looked at him, realizing that the question she had been expecting for weeks was on the tip of his tongue, and she was not prepared to answer it.

"I think it's best if I just speak plainly," he said, abandoning all efforts at romance. Ruth had already decided Arthur was not the romantic type and she was disappointed by that realization, but she tried to tell herself other things were more important, given their situation.

"Arthur, it will soon be dark," she said in a rush. "I need to get home. Could we talk about this tomorrow?"

"I need to say it now. Will you marry me?"

The question fell into the tense silence as he stared bleakly at Ruth. She stared back, unable to respond.

"I wish our circumstances were different. If we were in Victoria, I would take you to the gardens, we would have tea and a lovely meal. But we aren't in Victoria," he sighed, "we're in a rough mining town where half the town may starve before the winter is out. The other half may freeze to death. I want to protect you. I think it only makes sense for us to be together through this, don't you agree?"

Ruth sighed, dropping her gaze to the floor. She had considered, more than once, accepting his proposal when it came; but now that it had, she felt no excitement, not even a tiny spark of pleasure over the prospect of marrying him.

"Arthur," she said, choosing her words carefully, "I'm afraid I cannot commit to marriage just because it makes sense." Slowly, she lifted her eyes and looked at him, pleading with him to understand. "I would like to think that if we were in Victoria, enjoying the beauty, cast in a different mood, a different atmosphere, I might be more inclined to accept your proposal. But. . ." She couldn't bring herself to reject his proposal; the words were too difficult. Yet she didn't need to say more for he seemed to understand. She watched the disappointment slip over his features. "I want you to know I have the highest respect for you," she quickly added. "I admire your work, and I like being your nurse."

He sighed heavily and looked at her with sadness. "So what is the problem, aside from our having to be practical? And we do have to be practical, Ruth. We are in a very difficult situation here, one that is not likely to improve until the winter ends. People are marrying for less important reasons—to have a roof over their head, for example, or the assurance of food for the winter."

She nodded. "I know that. But you see, Arthur, I already have a roof over my head and food for the winter. For that reason, I do not feel compelled to rush into a lifelong commitment simply because it seems the logical thing to do." She took a deep breath. "I need something more than that, Arthur. And I'm not saying I won't find it with you. It's just that the timing is wrong."

His expression brightened. "I see what you're saying, and I think you have a valid point. We do not want to make a decision in haste. You owe that to your father, and I owe it to Katherine's memory, as well."

Ruth nodded, aware that Arthur still grieved over Katherine. That was the other thing. She did not want to be a rebound romance, someone who was grabbed in desperation to fill a lonely void in a man's heart. She wanted to be loved based on who she was as a person. She wanted the kind of love that was built on Christian principles and based on respect and need, but she also wanted to feel a glow in her heart. Furthermore, she wanted to look in the mirror and see joy in her eyes, the joy that she had seen on her mother's face. Perhaps it was an unlikely dream, given her circumstances; perhaps that kind of love didn't come to everyone. Perhaps her parents got lucky.

"We'll talk about this at another time," Arthur said tactfully. "Now shall I walk you home?"

Ruth looked out. It was almost seven o'clock and completely dark. The hours had flown by during the afternoon, as the clinic had been overflowing with patients and she couldn't abandon Arthur. But now, looking out, she knew better than to venture down the streets alone, with so many miners and drifters overflowing the saloons, hungry for a woman—any woman.

"Yes, Arthur, I would appreciate your walking me home."

He seemed grateful to be awarded the opportunity.

"Bear in mind," he said as they trudged back in the cold, "that I have the funds to buy your house, and we could set up a better clinic there. There wouldn't be any major adjustments for you. You would be working in the same surroundings as with your father. It could be very simple, Ruth. Very uncomplicated."

"And very practical," she said, trying to see his face through the cold darkness. "Maybe it's absurd, Arthur, but it just seems a bit too practical." She sighed. "I suppose I'm a foolish romantic who has read too many Dickens' novels. I'll take into consideration what you have said to me this evening. And I want you to know that I am flattered that you care enough for me to marry me."

"Thank you," he said, pressing her arm gently as they climbed the steps to her front porch.

Arthur had never touched her, other than linking his arm through hers to assist her in maneuvering her way over the uneven boards of the sidewalk, to ascend the steps. This time it was different. As he took her key and unlocked the door, he reached out for her, impulsively it seemed, and planted a cold kiss on her lips.

Ruth tried to respond but found it impossible. She merely smiled and touched his cheek with her gloved hand. "Good night," she said as she stepped inside and closed the door. Quickly, she lit the lantern in the hall, trying to ward off the terrible thought that had rushed to the foreground of her confused mind.

Arthur had kissed her and she felt nothing. Joe Spencer had merely looked at her and her heart had started to beat faster. Furthermore, when she was with Joe, something stirred in her soul, something responded in a way she could neither understand nor rationalize. Feelings; how strange and deceptive they were. How could she pass up a man who cared for her, who had so much to offer her for the hope of a man who had offered nothing, not even proof that he had any feelings for her beyond a polite friendship?

# seven

Joe and Ivan had worked together for weeks in the bitter cold, the only sound between them the creak of the windlass that passed from beneath the frozen ground to the top. Their hard labor had begun to pay off, however, for on the snow-covered ground there had been piles of gold-filled gravel days before. Now the gold had been filtered out, sacked up in bags, waiting to be taken into Dawson. At last there would be money to reward them for their efforts.

"Don't you want to go into town with me tomorrow?" Joe asked Ivan as they wearily spooned up their beans that evening.

Ivan shook his head. "I do not like people."

Joe chewed his food, staring across at the big man whose bald head gleamed in the glow of the lantern. "Then I'll collect the money and return."

Ivan looked across at him, saying nothing.

"Do you trust me?" Joe asked.

Ivan nodded, turning back to his beans.

❧

The next day as Joe rode into Dawson loaded down with a bulky pack of laundry and his rifle, he was shocked by the mood of melancholy that enveloped the town. The sight of thin dogs and slab-ribbed mules first greeted him. Then he noticed the grim-faced men moving briskly toward their tents. Scraping the mud and sand of the Yukon from his boots, he opened the door of the Alaska Commercial Company, where the tension of the town was being verbalized.

"It's the truth!" a voice bellowed as Joe entered.

The clerk behind the board counter had the gathering of men around the potbellied stove captivated.

"Ya mean to tell us," an older gentleman spoke up, "that if we'd taken free passage to Fort Yukon, the same thing could have happened to us?"

"Sure could of," the clerk answered.

"Hello." A female voice spoke up behind him.

Joe turned and looked down at Ruth Wright, standing directly behind him. Removing his hat, he smoothed down his hair and wondered about the rugged state of his appearance.

"Hello. How are you?" He smiled at her.

She looked as though she had lost more weight, although it was difficult to tell, for she was bundled in a black woolen cloak. Still, her cheeks were hollow and the shine was gone from her wide-set hazel eyes.

"I'm okay," she answered in a firm voice. "And you?"

The raucous conversation practically drowned out their words. Glancing back at the men then at Ruth, he took her elbow and they walked toward a quiet area in the rear of the store.

"I just got to town," he said, glancing at the men whose faces were flushed with emotion. "Could you tell me what they're discussing? Everyone seems to be upset."

Ruth nodded, glancing back at the group. "This fall the *Weare* dropped its fare to fifty dollars per person with the hope of encouraging some of the residents here to leave for the winter. We're already short of everything from food to supplies. When only a small number of people left on the *Weare*, the government offered free passage on the *Bella* to anyone who would leave Dawson and winter in Fort Yukon."

Her eyes returned to him, and she looked even sadder than before. "Unfortunately, the *Weare* couldn't get through the ice blocks near Fort Yukon. Passengers were loaded into small boats, but even those were blocked by the ice. Finally, the people anchored the boats at the edge of the forest, got out, and walked for three days to reach Fort Yukon. When they arrived, frozen and starved, they discovered a shortage of food there, just as here."

Joe shook his head. "That's terrible." He glanced back at the group of men who had become silent, staring glumly into space.

"What Mr. Carson was saying when you walked in was that some of those people who reached Fort Yukon pulled guns on the clerks at the Alaska Commercial Company there and demanded clothes and food. I guess they were desperate."

Joe had been listening to her words, while mentally sighing with relief that he now had gold to outfit himself and Ivan.

"What about you?" he asked suddenly. "Are you okay? Do you need anything?"

She looked startled by his question for a moment; then she shook her head and tried to smile at him. "No, I have enough. What about you?"

"I'm fine," he answered, looking into her troubled eyes. Her question and the concern in her eyes melted his heart. He forgot everything he had told himself about why he wouldn't bother to see her on this trip. She was standing before him, speaking to him in that kind voice that seemed to reach to the depths of his soul. A surge of tenderness for her rushed back.

"Look, I believe I owe you a meal or two. Is there any place in town that serves decent food?"

She smiled, a bit more cheerfully this time. "I do."

"I agree. You serve the best. What I had in mind was treating *you* this time—unless there's some reason you can't join me," he added, remembering Dr. Bradley.

She shook her head, and the hood toppled back onto her

shoulders. He couldn't resist staring at her lush auburn hair.

"No, as it happens, I left the clinic early. I'm helping Dr. Bradley," she explained quickly.

Joe did not respond to the reference to her work. He wanted to keep the conversation away from his competition.

જ

Ruth bathed and dressed for her date with Joe—*date?* she wondered. Her hand hesitated on her black silk dress as she pondered the question. Was this really a date? They were simply having a meal together, the voice of logic argued. Nevertheless, Joe had invited her out for a meal. In Seattle, that would be considered a date.

Humming softly to herself, she finished dressing then turned before the mirror, surveying her reflection. She was still grieving for her father, of course, and wore black; but she decided to forgo the usual dress of flannel, which most women in Dawson now wore for warmth, and chose instead a black woolen dress that was tucked at the bodice and hugged her narrow waist, showing off her good figure. She had lost weight and the dress was a bit loose through the shoulders, but it didn't matter.

Tilting her head, she studied her face. The loss of weight made her hazel eyes seem larger than ever; and although her complexion was quite pale, when she pinched her cheeks and bit her lips, a faint pink touched her skin.

Suddenly, she thought of her mother, and she knew her father had been right. With the unusual heart shape of her face and the thick auburn hair, she knew she very much resembled her mother when she was young.

She opened her small jewelry box and withdrew the cameo that had belonged to her mother. As it lay in the palm of her hand, she thought of how she and her father had both been cheated by the loss of such a lovely woman. Yet, the memories of her parents would always live in her heart.

Opening the clasp of the cameo, she placed the pin at the neck of her dress. It was the perfect complement to offset the stark black of the dress. Smoothing back the strands of her hair into its thick chignon, she turned from the mirror and began to speculate about her evening with Joe.

❧

The dining room of Mrs. Taylor's restaurant was a large, square room with six tables, four chairs to a table. The plain wooden tables were overlaid with tan linen cloths, and the bone china and silver cutlery were nice reminders of the homes so many people had left behind.

Joe pulled back a chair for her and she spread her skirts as she took a seat. He was wearing a fresh white shirt and dark trousers.

"Everything else that I own has been left at the laundry." He smiled across at her.

She nodded. A Tlingit family ran the local laundry, and she was always amazed at the enormous amount of work they managed. "They're very particular with the clothes," she said.

But she was not thinking of the people or the laundry as she looked across the candlelit table to him. His blond hair was slicked back from his bronzed face, and tonight his blue eyes seemed larger than ever and were the nicest shade of blue she had ever seen.

"Please excuse the length of my hair," he spoke up, as though her staring might be due to some fault on his part. "I haven't had time to visit a barber."

"There's only one good one that I know about here," she said, folding her hands in her lap. She gave the man's name and the location of his small log cabin. Many of the inhabitants of Dawson operated businesses out of their homes.

Mrs. Taylor appeared at their table, announcing that tonight's menu would be baked salmon, rice, dried apricots, canned tomatoes, and tapioca pudding. While she varied her menu each evening, she served family style to everyone.

"That sounds fine." Joe looked across at Ruth.

"Yes, it does," she agreed.

After Mrs. Taylor had left the table, the two sat staring for a moment, then Ruth cleared her throat.

"How are you doing with your claim?" she asked.

"It's going well," he said.

&

Joe stared at her for a moment, thinking. Should he tell her? He hadn't been to the assayer yet, but he knew the claim would probably make him rich. Ivan had said that gold salted with black sand was worth eleven dollars an ounce. "We completed our shaft and have been windlassing a ton of mud and gravel." He paused, glancing around the small dining room. "I brought in a sample," he said quietly.

"I hope it proves to be profitable."

"Thank you." As he looked at her, he kept wondering about what she was going to do. "How are you doing? I know I asked you that earlier, but I mean. . .how are you really doing? I've been worried about you."

She sighed. "Yes, it has been difficult."

"You must miss your father very much."

"I do." Then she took a deep breath and looked at him. "How is Kenai?"

He grinned. "Hungry. Do you have any idea how much malamutes eat?"

"No," she laughed.

"Actually, Kenai has been a great deal of company to me and to Ivan. In fact, Ivan needs him more than I do, I think. Ivan's a loner who doesn't trust people very much. Kenai is exactly the kind of companion he prefers."

Their food was delivered on pretty plates, served attractively, and Joe cast a longing glance at the crusty hot bread placed before them.

"I'm glad you invited me to eat with you," Ruth said.

Joe glanced across at her and saw that her hazel eyes held a glow again, and he was glad.

"I'm glad you could join me," he answered, picking up his fork. When he looked back at her, he saw that her eyes were closed for a moment before she reached for and unfolded her napkin.

"I must seem very rude," he said, "digging into my food without saying grace."

"No," she said with a smile. "You just seem like a hungry man."

"I am that," he answered, and they both laughed.

They were silent for a few minutes as they both enjoyed the food, then Joe put down his fork and looked at her. "You were right. The food here is very good, but I think you're the best cook in Dawson."

"Thank you," she answered. "When are you returning to camp?"

He sighed. "Tomorrow. Wish it were not so soon, but we're almost out of food, and we needed some mining supplies."

"Were you able to get what you needed at the mercantile today?" she asked.

"Not everything. There will be no more canned fruit until the boat comes in next spring. They're rationing sugar and coffee, as well. We can do without sugar, but we need the coffee to keep us alert." A sigh escaped him as he recalled the long, hard hours of work. Kerosene could no longer be obtained in Dawson, and now they would be working by the light of candles.

"Do you plan to stay in Dawson?" she asked. "I mean, after you strike it rich."

"I guess that depends on if I strike it rich," he said then laughed.

She tilted her head and looked at him thoughtfully, then she nodded slowly. "I think you will. You have the intelligence and determination."

"What about you?" he asked, watching her carefully. "You said you would probably leave, but that you might not return to Seattle." He was testing her, wondering if she would tell him about Arthur Bradley now. He had an almost overwhelming desire to know her plans, for he could no longer deny his feelings, although he had desperately tried.

"Why, Ruth!" A high-pitched voice turned his attention to the plump woman standing at their table, staring at him rather than Ruth. "How are you?"

Joe looked at Ruth and saw that her mouth had tightened, and her eyes seemed to have narrowed a bit. Something about this woman put Ruth's nerves on edge; that was obvious. As he looked back at the woman, he could see why. She was rudely gawking at both of them, and he wondered who she was. He didn't have to wonder long, for Ruth spoke up.

"Mrs. Greenwood, do you know Joe Spencer?"

Joe stood up and forced a smile. "I don't believe I've had the pleasure."

Her mouth dropped open as though taken aback by his response. He had noticed that not too many men here had manners; she seemed to be shocked by his response.

"This is Mrs. Greenwood," Ruth said as Mrs. Greenwood took in every inch of his clothing and even his boots, which he was glad he had just cleaned.

"Hello," she said.

"How do you do?" He tried to force a smile, although she

wasn't smiling; she was merely gawking at him.

Then the woman's large eyes shot back to Ruth. "How are you doing, dear?" The tone of her question made Joe suspect that she was probing for more than Ruth's health.

"I am well, thank you," Ruth said, looking uncomfortable as Mrs. Greenwood lingered at their table.

A silence followed, which Ruth did not bother to fill, so Joe sat back down in his chair.

"Well. . ." Mrs. Greenwood folded and unfolded her hands. "I'll be going. I just came to pick up a plate to take home to Mr. Greenwood. Nice meeting you." Her protruding eyes returned to Joe, boring through him once more before she turned around and pressed down her wide skirts to make the distance between two tables.

Joe looked across at Ruth and saw that her eyes were lowered. He wanted to ask about the woman, but Ruth didn't seem inclined to talk about her. He picked up his fork again, trying to remember where he had heard the name. Then it came to him. Miss Mattie at the boardinghouse had said that a Mrs. Greenwood had entertained Ruth and Bradley at her home for Thanksgiving.

As he pretended to concentrate on his food, he realized that what he had seen on Ruth's face now was embarrassment. If she were seeing Bradley, maybe she was embarrassed to be seen here with him. And yet, nothing about Ruth suggested that she would be dishonest or unfaithful once she was committed to someone.

Her heavy sigh caught his attention. "I'm afraid that by breakfast tomorrow everyone in Dawson will know that we had dinner together."

"Oh? And is that so bad?" he asked, his tone guarded.

She shook her head. "No, of course not. This is the first evening I've truly enjoyed." She sighed. "It's just that Mrs.

Greenwood is a bit of a busybody, and she seems to have taken me under her wing since Father died."

"So how does taking you under her wing affect my having dinner with you?" Suddenly, he was thinking about his past, wondering if Mrs. Greenwood would start asking questions. The very idea of that made him nervous, and his appetite began to wane.

She looked thoughtful for a moment. When her eyes returned to his face, the glow in her eyes was gone. "She thinks I should accept Bradley's proposal."

Her honesty caught him off guard, and for a moment he could only stare at her. What he saw in her eyes, however, lifted his spirits. At the mention of Bradley's name, there was no enthusiasm in her voice or in her eyes. At last, he had the opportunity to ask the question that had been troubling him.

"And how do you feel? Do you think you should accept his proposal?" His throat tightened on those words, and he found them difficult to speak, but he had to find out.

She shook her head. "No, I don't. In fact, I've already turned him down."

"You have?" His voice betrayed him again, and his eyes, too, he imagined. It was the best news he had heard since he had been in Dawson. To his surprise, he felt, at that very moment, Ruth Wright mattered even more to him than the gold. That frightened him.

She looked down at the bread in her hand. "I don't love him. In the Yukon, that doesn't seem to be a logical reason to decline a proposal. Widows are marrying the first respectable man who asks, some women are coming here from advertisements in newspapers, others are simply fortune hunters drifting in. . . ." Her words trailed as her cheeks colored.

The latter description was obviously a referral to the women who had set up shop on the back street in the world's oldest profession. He leaned back in the chair and looked at her.

"But you aren't like any of those women. You are a very special woman and you have a lot to offer. Don't settle for less than you want, Ruth. Don't let loneliness or hard times force you into a commitment that would not make you happy."

She looked up at him. Her eyes softened and she began to smile. "Thank you for speaking words I very much needed to hear. You see, I feel I would be cheating the other person as much as myself. Maybe I'm just a romantic at heart, but if I can't enter into a commitment that brings me happiness and joy, I'd prefer to remain single. I'm speaking very personally," she added, looking away. "It's just that Mrs. Greenwood and—"

"And Arthur Bradley, I imagine—"

"Yes. They think I should be considering my security and safety. I am constantly reminded that it is unsafe for a single woman to live in a large house, as I do, where medicine has been kept and where so many desperate people have come to our door. Some of those men have been out in the bush and don't know my father has died."

He leaned forward, pushing his plate away, concerned for her now. He hadn't considered the importance of what she was saying, and he felt like a fool for not having thought of it.

"That does make sense," he said. "I mean, about your safety. But you don't have to marry someone just to insure your safety. Why don't you take in boarders? Some of these other widows you just mentioned. It seems to me they should be banding together with each other rather than jumping at the first offer to marry a man, when many of those men will be out in the bush half the time, anyway. Unless they're merchants," he added, "which would make more sense."

"I thought about it," she said, nodding slowly. "But the truth is, I enjoy being alone. I suppose that's a selfish attitude, but I can last until spring on my own, and I do know how to use a gun," she added with a little smile. "I'm quite certain I could never bring myself to use that gun, but it poses a threat."

His mind was still lodged on the knowledge that there was some merit to Mrs. Greenwood and Bradley's argument about her being alone in her particular situation. "It's a large house for Dawson. Surely you could find one or two respectable women who could live with you, and there should be enough room."

"There is," she said, touching the linen napkin to her lips. She, too, had lost interest in the meal. "And you have a very good idea. I'll give that some serious thought tomorrow."

He was pleased to see that her eyes looked more hopeful now. For a moment, he feared Mrs. Greenwood had destroyed their evening.

"Good." He couldn't resist thinking about how it would be to come in from the mines to her home, to be there with her, enjoy her companionship as he was doing now. Just as quickly, he pushed the thought aside. What was wrong with him? He couldn't allow himself to fall in love with Ruth Wright. He was here on a mission, and he couldn't for one moment forget it.

"Thank you for inviting me to dinner," she said as a waiter came to clear away their dishes.

"It's been my pleasure, I assure you. Ivan doesn't make a very good dinner companion," he added, wanting to change the subject.

"Christmas Day is only two weeks away," she said, looking around the restaurant. The sparse decorations in town practically ignored the season, but Ruth was determined to celebrate it as always. "Will you be returning to Dawson over the holidays?"

He frowned. "I'm ashamed to admit that I hadn't even thought about it."

"You have a lot on your mind," she acknowledged. "I just wanted to say that if you do, I'd be happy to share my Christmas meal with you."

"That's very nice of you," he said, genuinely touched. "Are you saying you'll be alone?"

She sighed. "I imagine Mrs. Greenwood will invite me to her house."

He grinned at her. "You don't seem too enthused by that."

She said nothing; she merely smiled at him, but her eyes said it all.

"In that case, I'll make it a point to return to town to spend Christmas Day with you. In fact, I'll look forward to it."

Her eyes brightened. "I can't promise turkey, but I will do my best to have a meal comparable to the traditional feast."

"Just being with you will be special enough," he said, and for a moment their eyes locked.

She blinked and glanced down at her plate then back at him. "There'll be a special church service that evening. Would you like to accompany me?"

He hesitated. In all honesty, he had to admit he had enjoyed the last service, and he knew some spiritual growth was needed in his life. "Yes, I would be happy to attend."

She smiled and suddenly looked relieved. "Good."

He glanced around and realized the dining room was emptying.

"Does Mrs. Taylor have a designated hour for closing?" he asked.

Ruth glanced around the room. "About now, I think." She looked back at him and they both laughed. The time had flown by.

"Shall we go?" He stood up and came around to hold her chair. His eyes moved from her narrow shoulders to her tiny waist. She had lost quite a bit of weight since he first met her.

Was it from lack of food, or did she miss her father that much?

A new resolve settled over him. If he could make this woman happy, he was certainly going to try. He might not ever meet anyone like her again. He was glad he had accepted her invitation to return for Christmas and attend church services.

He paid the ticket, six dollars for two meals, which might have been considered steep to some, but to him it had been a bargain. He decided to at least share that thought with her.

"This is the first meal I've enjoyed since my last one at your home." He took her elbow and steered her back to the coat tree beside the door. As he helped her into her heavy cloak, his hands lingered on her shoulders for a second, and he found himself desperately wanting to put his arms around her, shield her from the night cold they were about to face. Instead, he forced himself to reach for his coat and hat.

"Then you should eat here again," she said as he opened the door for her and they stepped onto the boardwalk.

"I think the company increased my enjoyment of the meal. So if I eat here again, I would need for you to join me."

Her laughter flowed into the soft darkness. "I think I could manage to do that."

They sauntered along, following the dim patches of light from the candles in windows decorated with pine cones and colorful bows. Joe was grateful for the short walk to her house, for he found himself thinking of her safety again as his eyes darted to open alleyways and the shadows of men leaning against a building farther down the street.

"Do you go out much?" he asked, tightening his grip on her arm.

"I only go out alone during the four to five hours of daylight."

"What about to and from the clinic?" he asked, frowning.

"Arthur walks with me," she said in a quiet voice.

"I see." He was sure Bradley was more than happy for a

chance to be with her, and he was suddenly fighting jealousy; but he told himself to stop behaving like an idiot and be glad for Ruth's safety. He was glad there was a man to see her home.

"One really has to adjust to daylight and darkness here," she said in a pleasant tone, as though she had long since conquered the problem. "At first the long daylight hours were such a novelty," she said and leaned against his arm. "When we arrived in midsummer, we had twenty hours of daylight, and the days seemed to go on forever. I had difficulty going to bed when it was still light outside, but I solved the problem by covering my bedroom window with dark flannel." She laughed softly, and her breath made a tiny circle of fog before her mouth as the cold air pierced their faces. "Now, I move around the house with a lantern in my hand most of the time."

"Do you still have a supply of kerosene?"

"Yes, I'm fortunate there. Father was wise enough to stock us up on the most important basics. I'm grateful for that. I'm afraid I was quite ignorant about what we needed here."

They had reached her front porch, but she seemed inclined to continue the conversation. "The editor of the Seattle paper published a letter for all people heading for the Klondike. The letter was a real blessing. The letter was from a woman in Skagway and listed the provisions a person should have before even considering a trip here. We followed her list precisely, even to my purchase of knickers to wear under skirts. It was a wise suggestion," she added, laughing softly as they climbed the steps.

Joe remembered noticing the things most people referred to as bloomers peeking from under women's dresses, and he saw the practicality of those in such cold country.

"I suppose you were accustomed to fancy petticoats and such," he said, grinning at her.

She laughed at that. They were standing at the door, and she hesitated.

"You don't need to feel compelled to invite me in for a cup of tea," he said quickly. "Not that you would," he added, hoping he hadn't sounded too presumptuous.

"Take care of yourself, Joe Spencer," she said, reaching for his hand.

Through their gloves, he could feel her firm grip and marveled at the courage of this remarkable woman. That thought prompted him to squeeze her hand gently.

"Thank you, Ruth. Please be careful," he added, feeling more protective of her than ever. "In fact," he looked at the dim light through the front window, "if you will allow me, I'd like to come in and check out the house for you. I'll wait until you've lit more candles."

"All right," she said, turning to unlock the door. "That's a very considerate thing for you to do, Joe."

As he entered the quiet, dim house, he found himself suddenly thinking of Mrs. Greenwood and he glanced over his shoulder. He felt certain that at the moment she was probably peering through a window somewhere, wondering if Ruth was safe with him tonight.

The hallway echoed the hollow steps of his boots as he walked to the clinic, checking the locked door. He turned and looked up and down the hall, and as he did, he realized how quiet and lonely the house felt. He turned to Ruth, who was removing her cloak and placing it on the coat tree.

"You know, you are a very brave woman," he said, voicing the thought that had been uppermost in his mind. "I'm afraid I hadn't given much thought to your situation here. It's good that you have friends who do think of that and are concerned for you."

She shook her hair back and he stared at the rich auburn

color highlighted by the glow of the lantern on the table. "I'm afraid Mrs. Greenwood is more concerned than I'd like her to be," she said, looking perplexed. "But I know she means well, and I must continue to remind myself of that."

"Let me check the upstairs for you," he said, glancing at the stairs that rose into darkness. "You can wait here, if you like."

Ruth looked at him and felt a bit of relief in having someone other than Arthur looking out for her. "All you'll find is a few tumbled rooms," she called after him.

She still kept the house immaculate, for she had little else to do to occupy her time, but she hadn't been able to force herself to go through her father's things to sort through and select what should be kept and what should be donated. She had begun the process but then stopped halfway, and now there were books stacked in little piles all over the living room floor.

She could hear his footsteps overhead, slow and deliberate, as he moved from room to room. He was a kind and caring man, she decided, and this made her feel better about her undeniable attraction toward him. Her father had said they didn't know him very well, and that had been true at the time. Now, however, she felt she knew him as well as anyone else in Dawson. Or rather, she knew him well enough to allow her heart to take the chance.

Hugging her arms against her, trying to offset the chill of the downstairs, she watched as his long legs descended the stairs; then her eyes moved upward to the broad chest in the white shirt and lingered on the gold sheen of his hair. As she met the deep blue eyes, her heart beat faster, and she turned to adjust the wick on the lantern.

"Everything looks fine," he said, as he reached her side again. "Do me the favor of inviting a lady to share the house with you, please. Otherwise, I'm going to worry about you."

She turned from the lantern and looked into his eyes.

"Thank you. It's comforting to know that you care."

"I do care," he said quickly.

She must have taken a step closer to him without realizing it, for he was suddenly standing very near to her. Or had he moved when she did?

He reached for her hand, and as her palms touched the thickness of his fur gloves, she could sense the strong masculinity of him, and for a moment, her thoughts flew wildly. She found herself wondering what it would be like to take shelter in his arms, rest her head against his broad chest, and feel the safety everyone felt she needed. More important to her was the opportunity to offset the terrible loneliness that engulfed her at times.

Had her thoughts brought the action about, or had he read something in her face and reached for her? Suddenly, she was standing with her head against his chest. She could feel the strength in his arms, and yet he was a gentle man. She sighed, unable to resist the pleasure of just having someone hold her. No, not just *someone*. It was Joe Spencer she wanted.

"I'd better go," he said, breaking into her thoughts.

She looked up into his face, half in shadow now with his back to the lantern. She tried to read the expression in his blue eyes for she longed to know how he really felt for her. As she stood looking up into his face, his lips brushed hers in a sweet gentle kiss. And for the first time in her life, she had an inkling of what real romance was. . .a friendship then a kiss, a kiss that brought a feeling of joy and longing to be near that person. Always.

But already he was withdrawing from her, stepping back, looking deep into her eyes. For a moment, neither of them spoke, then he took a deep breath. "I must go," he said.

"Thank you for a lovely evening," she said, amazed that her voice was calm despite the rapid beat of her heart. "And I hope you'll stop in the next time you come to Dawson," she added.

"Yes, I will." He headed for the door, and her eyes followed him, watching as he replaced the felt hat on his golden head. "Ruth. . ." He turned slowly and looked at her.

"Yes?" She waited anxiously, desperately wanting him to speak words of reassurance, words that would let her know he felt the same way she did.

"Take care of yourself," he finally replied.

"Thanks. You, too." She smiled, following him to the door. Her hopes were already sinking, but she tried to cover her disappointment. During the ten minutes he had been inside the house, he could have been any other well-meaning friend or neighbor. Except for the kiss. Surely, he realized she didn't allow just anyone to kiss her; it had been a very personal thing for her. How did he feel?

He smiled at her then stepped out, closing the door softly. She turned the key in the latch then leaned against the door, pressing her head against the cold wood.

What if he didn't feel the way she did? What if his heart wasn't beating in the same crazy rhythm as hers? She couldn't bear to think he didn't share her feelings. She hugged her arms around her, feeling cold and lonely again as she climbed the stairs. Maybe there was no future with Joe Spencer, but she would prefer one sweet memorable evening with him to a lifetime with Arthur Bradley, bless his heart.

❧

As Joe walked back to Miss Mattie's Roadhouse in the cold darkness, thoughts flew about his brain like pesky mosquitoes in summer. It had taken every ounce of self-discipline not to take her in his arms and kiss her again and again. Still, she was a lady and a very good one at that. A Christian lady, he added, recalling their hour in the prayer service.

Shoving his hands into his coat pockets, trying to absorb some warmth, he tried to sort through his feelings. He cared for her more than any woman he had ever met in his life, and he knew that now. She was a strong woman, yet kind and gentle; she was not a whiner or a complainer, even though she had reason to complain. Life had not been fair to her; that much was obvious to him. She had lost her mother when she was young. Then she had obviously passed up a comfortable life in Seattle and many suitors, no doubt, to come to Dawson with her father. She had said it was his dream. Or maybe he said that. In any case, he knew Ruth Wright had come here for her father's benefit rather than her own.

He recalled his first conversation with the two of them. "We didn't come here to get rich," she had said in a quiet yet firm voice. "We came to help those who would obviously be in need of medical care."

And they had. It seemed a cruel twist of fate that her father had been taken at a crucial time, leaving her alone to survive the winter. But even at that, she seemed to be attempting to hide her tears, and she was obviously determined to cope.

He had reached the boardinghouse, but he felt inclined to linger outside for a moment and stare up at the stars. The sky was a dark canvas with bright glittering stars and only a half moon. The air was very clear here in the north, and it did him good to look up at the vast sky and study the handiwork of God.

*The handiwork of God.* That kind of thought had not crossed his mind in a long time.

He sighed and turned for the door. Ruth was good for him in many ways. He longed to stay on for a few days, spend more time with her, follow the strong pull of his heart toward Ruth Wright and see where it led.

A deep sigh wrenched his body as reality pushed through

his fogged brain. There was gold waiting to be assayed, and supplies to be bought, and a claim to be worked. He couldn't get soft now; the timing was all wrong.

With that in mind, he entered the boardinghouse and forced himself to think of tomorrow and what must be done.

# eight

Ruth had taken Joe's concern more seriously than that of Mrs. Greenwood and Arthur Bradley. Before going to sleep, she had prayed for the right person with whom to share her home.

Her answer came the first of the week, when a woman appeared at her front door, with a thin pale face peering from beneath a thick, black hooded cape.

"Good morning," she said. "My name is Dorie Farmer. Miss Mattie at the boardinghouse said one of her guests suggested you might be interested in taking in a lady boarder."

The *boarder* who had suggested this to Miss Mattie, of course, was Joe, and Ruth smiled at that, as she looked at the woman before her. She was a tall woman who appeared to be in her mid-thirties. Her face was plain with the exception of keen brown eyes that reflected intelligence and curiosity as she looked at Ruth. Beneath the thick cloak, Ruth could see this woman was dressed in the most liberal fashion of the day—a shorter skirt, ankle length, that revealed thick flannel bloomers above rubber boots, crusted with mud. As Ruth's eyes swept back up the dark, serviceable cape, she saw the dirt stains on it as well.

"I know I must look a sight," the woman said, glancing down at her clothing. "But if you understand that I walked over Chilkoot Pass—"

"Chilkoot Pass?" Ruth gasped.

It was one of the worst journeys a man could make to Dawson; Ruth couldn't imagine a woman making this tortuous journey, even though some had arrived by that route during milder weather.

Ruth opened the door wider. "Come in. You must be half-frozen."

"Thank you. First, I'll remove these filthy boots." Dorie Farmer stepped out of her boots, and Ruth glimpsed a pair of moccasins underneath as the woman stepped inside and looked around. "I hear you have the nicest home in Dawson, and I can see this is true."

"Thank you," Ruth said. "May I take your cloak?"

"Yes, please." The woman removed her fur gloves and stuffed them in the pockets of the cloak. Then she removed the cloak as her eyes slowly moved over the interior of the house. "I understand this was a clinic," she said, carelessly patting down her thin brown hair, streaked with gray on the sides and worn in a loose chignon.

"It was," Ruth nodded, hanging the cloak on the coat tree. "My father and I came to Dawson back in the summer. He passed away recently."

Dorie Farmer nodded. "I heard that," she said, speaking gently. "I'm so sorry. Are you still running the clinic?"

The question took Ruth by surprise. Unlike everyone else who expected her to shut down, which indeed she had, this woman seemed to think it was possible for Ruth to run the clinic on her own.

"No," she replied, shaking her head. "I'm a nurse, not a doctor. I do assist the other doctor here in his clinic."

"I see. Well, you'll find that I am curious by nature. It accompanies my profession."

"Which is?" Ruth asked with a smile. It was easy to be frank with this woman.

"I'm a correspondent for the San Francisco *Examiner,*" she answered. "I'll probably write a few articles for the Klondike

*Nugget* here, as well."

"How fascinating!" All sorts of questions were rushing into Ruth's mind, but then she remembered her manners. "Come upstairs and I'll make tea."

"Thank you very much. I haven't had a decent cup of tea since. . .well, I can't remember when. On the Pass, we were lucky to get enough snow melt for drinking water."

Ruth glanced back at her, still amazed that this woman had survived such a tortuous journey.

"Oh, this feels like home," Dorie said upon following Ruth through the living room to the kitchen. "May I wash my hands?"

Ruth pointed her toward the wash basin as she checked the water in the teakettle, relieved to see that there was enough and that it was still hot. She went to the cabinet for tea and cups.

"I'm in desperate need of a wash house. Can you refer me to one?"

Ruth considered offering the use of her tin tub, but remembering hygiene, forced herself to limit her generosity until she got to know Dorie Farmer better.

"There are two bath houses here," she said. "One offers spruce steam baths, and that is the one I would recommend. It's run by a Tlingit couple—"

"Oh, yes, the Tlingit," Dorie nodded. "They are so wise and practical. We had Tlingit guides leading us over the Pass. I'm certain we would never have survived without them."

Ruth nodded. "They know the area well, since they were the first inhabitants. The people who run the bath house I mentioned learned about the proper bath system from an American living in Skagway. Like the people who run the laundry, they are very clean and take pride in their equipment. I think you'll be as comfortable as you can be, given the choices." Then she tilted her head and looked at Dorie with the eye of a nurse. "Are you feeling all right? Malnutrition and scurvy are common maladies of the journey here."

"I've been fortunate, thank you," Dorie smiled. "I brought my own cache of herbs and dried fruits, which have saved my life more than once since leaving San Francisco a year ago—"

"A year ago?" Ruth asked, surprised by this.

"Yes, I've spent the past year interviewing miners, travelers, anyone and everyone who could tell me something about this country—those who had lived here and those who wanted to get rich here. I first disembarked at Juneau and spent some time there. Then I caught a boat to Skagway and got stranded there for the winter. At spring breakup I went the ten miles to Dyea. My ultimate goal was Dawson, and to get here I knew the most entertaining route would be over Chilkoot or White Pass, but I chose Chilkoot, since there seemed to be more stories circulating about that one."

"So you climbed over that steep pass to get stories for your paper?"

"That's right. I guess I sound pretty crazy, but then I had to wonder about my sanity when I ended up wintering in Skagway. It's a disorderly little place but not really as notorious as it's made out to be. Grant you, there are shootings day and night, but I'm afraid I've used that to my advantage. My job is entertaining people back in San Francisco. Shameful, isn't it?"

Ruth looked at her. In a way, she thought it was; but this woman was so honest about herself and her job that she couldn't help liking her.

"Well, I'm sure you've met lots of interesting people in your travels."

"I have. And I've been greatly inspired by those who left everything behind to follow their dream of striking it rich. So many have died in the process," she said on a heavy sigh. "But there *are* many interesting stories. And you'd be amazed at the number of enterprising women who have followed their husbands and ended up getting rich through their own ingenuity in supplying what was needed in camps and tent towns."

Ruth nodded. "There's a woman here in Dawson who's making a nice income simply by selling hot water bottles to miners and silk cloth to the women who were desperately homesick for the nice things they left behind."

"That's the kind of ingenuity I mean. This woman was smart enough to think of that, you see. Maybe I'll interview her for a story!" Dorie's brown eyes brightened as she shook the dripping water from her hands into the basin.

Ruth handed her a cup towel. "I can see that you're going to liven up my lonely house," Ruth said. "I can't wait to talk with you. You must have lots of stories to tell."

Dorie dried her hands and studied Ruth with an amused grin. "You've decided to take me on as a boarder, then?"

"Of course," Ruth smiled, motioning her to a chair. On an impulse, she went to the cabinet and got down a tin of tea cakes that she reserved for special occasions, now that she was having to ration herself on everything she ate.

"Tea cakes!" Dorie clasped her hands together before her gallused shirt, looking as delighted as a child on Christmas morning. "Do you have any idea how long it's been since I had anything resembling a delicacy? Beans and hardtack, and the occasional smoked fish. I may never eat those three items again," she said, taking a seat.

Ruth laughed, delighted by her new boarder. She knew that Dorie was an answer to her prayers. Suddenly the long winter stretching before her didn't seem so bad. Then she had another thought. "How long did you want to stay?"

Dorie shrugged, lifting her teacup. "Hard to say. Everyone's telling me we're frozen in here for the winter, but I don't know if I can stay in one place that long."

"I'm afraid your destinations are limited, unless you want to go out to the mining camps to interview the miners."

"Oh, I already spent some time at one camp, and I plan to go to others," Dorie said after a generous sip of tea.

Ruth's eyebrows rose. She had merely been teasing, but she saw that Dorie was perfectly serious.

"Makes for the kind of reading folks back in San Francisco want," she explained, reaching for a tea cake.

Ruth sipped her tea, recalling the mood of her hometown before she left. "Yes, I remember that everyone in Seattle was wild to hear news of the Klondike."

"So you and your father just arrived this summer?"

"In the height of mosquito season," Ruth said, shaking her head. "I will be forever grateful to an article in our newspaper about the importance of taking mosquito netting for hats and gloves to protect the hands."

"I wrote a similar article for my newspaper, only I'm afraid I did more complaining than warning. I've had some unpleasant run-ins with those varmints," Dorie said, then looked at Ruth with a blissful smile. "This tea cake is manna from heaven. But speaking of mosquitoes, I don't remember them being as much a challenge as trying to survive the Chilkoot."

Ruth leaned forward. "How on earth did you survive that awful journey at this time of year? In fact, I thought the Pass was already closed down."

"We were the last people over it." She sighed. "I hope I can blot from my memory some of the terrible things that happened along the way. Dogs and horses dropping dead from exhaustion, people lying down in the snow, begging God to let them go on and freeze. It was awful," she said, looking seriously at Ruth.

Ruth's mouth fell open, and for a moment she couldn't even visualize such horror. "I've been spared those atrocities," she said. "We've had lots of patients as a result of climbing one of the passes. They've come in with pneumonia, rheumatism, or scurvy, and in one case all three. However, most of those people were so sick and weary that they wanted to forget their experiences rather than discuss them."

"Which is what I should do," Dorie said, staring at Ruth's tablecloth.

Then with a chapped hand, she touched the tablecloth, trailing the balls of her fingers over the smooth linen. "You have no idea what a pleasure it is just to touch a nice tablecloth or press a cloth napkin to my mouth." Her brown eyes roamed over the kitchen. "Or to sit in the warmth and comfort of your kitchen. It seems as grand as a ballroom compared to the frozen campfire suppers or windblown tent kitchens."

Ruth smiled sadly. "I don't see how you did it. I imagine a soft bed will feel even better to you."

Dorie groaned. "There's nothing I can think of that appeals to me more. The softest thing I've put to my back is a board covered with clothing for a mattress."

"Is all that really worth the story?" Ruth asked, amazed that this woman had endured so much, having come from a nice city like San Francisco.

Dorie laughed. "I'm afraid being a correspondent is my obsession in life. Actually, it is my life. I've never been married, never even wanted to be. My work has meant everything to me."

"I've never been that enamored with nursing," Ruth sighed. "I enjoy helping sick people, and the satisfaction of seeing them restored to good health is a reward, but. . ." Her voice trailed. What she really wanted was to have a family, to be a wife and mother.

"Now tell me," Dorie said matter-of-factly, "will I be putting you out here? I'll be delighted to sleep on that sofa I saw in there." She indicated the living room with a wag of her head.

"I can put you up in my father's room, although I'll have to do some straightening up."

"Please don't trouble yourself," Dorie said. "If this is a painful task for you—after so recently losing your father, I mean—I will be more than happy to take care of that myself, if you instruct me how you want things done."

Ruth shook her head. "No, I can manage. In fact, I'll probably thank you later for giving me the incentive I needed to assemble those piles of books into some kind of order."

Dorie nodded then pressed her hands against the table and stood up slowly.

"Are you aching in your muscles or joints?" Ruth asked, suddenly feeling like a nurse again.

"Just a bit stiff. I'll get over it. May I call you Ruth? And of course I'm Dorie."

"Of course," Ruth smiled.

"Now, Ruth, I want to make it clear that I'll pull my share of the load. I'm accustomed to doing things that way. We can take turns washing dishes and cooking, if you like."

Ruth considered her suggestion. "For now, why don't you just take care of any business you have in town and let me handle the house?"

Dorie gave her a grateful smile. "I'm so appreciative of your kindness. I think God sent me directly to your door."

"Oh, I'm sure He did," Ruth answered quickly. "And I must remember to thank Joe for passing the word on."

"Who?"

"Joe Spencer. He's a friend who suggested I take in a boarder, although I didn't think I needed one."

Dorie nodded. "By the way, I haven't asked how much you charge."

Ruth hadn't even thought about it. "Having someone in the house with me is payment enough."

"Oh no." Dorie frowned, thoroughly rumpling her forehead again. "That's no way to do business, friend. I can pay you a dollar a day if that sounds fair."

"That's too much," Ruth said, even though she knew it was lower than Dorie would pay anywhere else in Dawson. Still, as she had said to Joe, she and her father had not come here to get rich.

"It's only fair," Dorie insisted. "I'm going to be eating with you, and I've already heard about the scarcity of groceries, so we have to be practical here."

Ruth hesitated. "All right. I will need boat passage in the spring, so I can use the money to start saving up for my fare."

"You're leaving then?"

For a fleeting moment, the image of Joe Spencer flashed through Ruth's mind. Still, she knew she could not plan her life around him unless there was reason to do so. "I'm planning to leave, yes."

"Don't blame you," Dorie said. "I'll probably be on the boat as well. When do they think the earliest passage might come about?"

Ruth thought of the conversations she had heard around town. "Most people think it will be late May before the Yukon thaws out enough for a boat to get through."

Dorie groaned. "And this is December. Sounds like forever. Well, I'm off to run some errands. Can I pick up anything for you?"

"No thanks." Ruth smiled. She was already feeling the relief of having someone to endure the winter with her, to help with food and errands, and offset the long, dark days and nights.

"Then I'm gone." At that, Dorie hurried out of the kitchen.

Ruth lingered at the table, listening to her footsteps flying down the stairs. She marveled that she had the energy to move after such a grueling journey.

As she took the cups and plates to the sink, she thanked God for sending Dorie Farmer to her door. And she added a word of thanks for Joe Spencer, as well. He was proving to be a blessing in her life, and she was grateful for that.

&

Joe had ridden back to camp with the good news that their claim was going to be a rich one. He had deposited almost three thousand dollars in their joint account and had given Ivan the deposit slip to prove the money had been deposited.

"Our supplies came to almost seven hundred dollars, doing the best I could to save us money," he explained.

"Robbers," Ivan grumbled. "The shopkeepers are robbers."

Joe sighed. "True, but without them, we couldn't mine and we'd starve to death, so we have to pay their prices."

"And they know it," Ivan fussed. He looked Joe over. "You are tired. I will unload," he said in his matter-of-fact way.

Kenai trotted up to lick Joe's hand, and he knelt, stroking the thick fur and looking into the dog's soulful eyes. "Someone asked about you, Kenai," Joe said softly. "A very pretty someone."

He petted Kenai for a few more minutes then dragged himself inside the cabin and collapsed on his cot. Every bone in his body ached from the hurried trip into Dawson and back and all the errands and business he had tried to cram into his short stay there.

Ruth slipped across his mind, a warm comfort as the wind howled about the eaves of the cabin. Stretching his aching legs, he closed his eyes. To offset the cold and the weariness in his bones, he allowed himself the pleasure of imagining her hazel eyes shining up into his and feeling the soft touch of her hand. He had practically fought himself to keep from touching her thick hair, and it had been an even greater struggle to keep from kissing her more than once.

He heaved a sigh. She was a fine wonderful woman but one he couldn't have. Or could he? First, he must come to grips with his personal life before he allowed himself to think about Ruth.

For the hundredth time, he longed to go back in time to that fateful night in Skagway. If only he had not been so stupid, so impulsive. The pain of regret stabbed him unmercifully, worse than any physical pain he had ever experienced. If only there was some way to change his past, to make amends. Then he could begin a new future with Ruth. . .well, at least he would be in a position to ask her. . .what? To marry him? Was that what he wanted? A future with Ruth?

Throughout the night, he tossed and turned, trying to sleep; but for most of the night, sleep eluded him. When he heard Ivan stumbling around, lighting candles, signaling it was time for their work day to begin, he regretted wasting precious rest time, trying to make sense of his life.

ka

Ruth had worked side by side with Arthur, busily caring for one patient after another until the day finally ended. They hadn't even stopped for lunch, only a quick cup of tea here and there throughout the day. When the last patient left, Ruth sank into a chair, exhausted.

"Ruth, it isn't fair to ask you to work these long, grueling hours," Arthur said.

"It isn't as though either of us has a choice, Arthur. Who else will tend these sick people? And they seem to be multiplying," she said, shaking her head as she stared into space.

He sighed, dropping his thin frame into the chair opposite

her. "I wish I had never come here," he said dully.

She frowned, focusing on him through eyes that ached with the need for sleep. "I know you have regrets about losing your wife, but are you saying you regret being a doctor here?"

He nodded. "I'm not cut out for this kind of work. Perhaps I would be happier in a hospital setting. I know for sure I can't bear this awful town."

Ruth listened to him and compared her own feelings with his as he spoke. "I don't mind Dawson that much, and I feel truly rewarded from caring for these people. I don't understand why you don't."

He shook his head. "I don't know, either. But I don't."

His mouth sagged with defeat, and his thin face looked pale and drawn.

"Arthur, I recall Father suggesting that you read Paul's epistles. Do you read your Bible at all now?"

He stared at the floor and shook his head. "No, I don't."

"I believe you would find comfort by reading the Bible. God will help you, Arthur, if only you'll turn to Him."

He lifted his face and looked at her. "He hasn't helped me much so far."

The bitterness in his voice shocked her. She was trying to find the right words to respond when he answered her thoughts.

"I lost my wife, and then when I met you, I hoped I might find happiness again. However," he sighed, returning his gaze to the floor, "you've made it quite clear that you have no interest in me whatsoever."

"That's not true. I *am* interested in you as a friend, Arthur. Can't we be friends?"

For several seconds he didn't answer. Then when he lifted his eyes to her, she saw the pain in his face.

"No, we can't be. You don't know what it's like," he said miserably, "working side by side with someone who can never belong to you. It's like looking through a shop window, seeing something bright and lovely, and wanting it with all of your heart. Then the truth cuts like a knife: You can never have what you want. Why, Ruth?" he said, his voice rising. "Why do you have to be so unreasonable? Can't you see that we should be together? That we could make each other happy?"

"No, I can't see that. And in time, I think you will find someone with whom you will be happy. But I'm not that someone."

"I think you are."

She thought he was being stubborn, but she was too weary to argue. She pushed herself out of the chair and walked to the coat tree. "I'm going home for the night. I think you need to get some rest, as well."

He stood and walked over to help her with her cloak, but then his arms lingered on her shoulder. "Ruth, please give me a chance," he said, turning her to face him.

"Arthur, there's no point in talking about this," she said, beginning to feel angry now that he was being so persistent.

Then he surprised her by pulling her against his chest and pressing his lips to hers.

Shocked, then angered even more, she put her hands on his chest and pushed him away.

"Don't ever touch me again," she said, glaring at him. "Until now, I have considered you a friend. But I'm not sure I think of you that way anymore."

She was out the door before he could say anything more. She started trudging home, not caring about the cold and the darkness or the fact that she was alone. Soon she heard footsteps racing up behind her, and Arthur had caught up.

"You shouldn't walk home alone," he said, stuffing his hands into the pockets of his overcoat.

She did not reply; she was still too angry. Quickening her steps, she said nothing to him until they reached her front porch. Looking up and seeing the lights in the window, she was more grateful than ever that Dorie Farmer was boarding with her.

"Good night," he said. "And again, I am sorry."

She turned back to him, having made a decision during the cold walk home. "Arthur, I've been thinking about what you said about the. . .difficulty of our working together. I think it's best if I resign from being your nurse. Mrs. Westhoover can help you. I believe she was a nurse a number of years ago in Toronto."

"But Ruth, I've apologized!"

She took a deep breath, feeling the cold air sting her lungs. "And I accept your apology. If you will be gracious about my resignation, I'm willing to keep what happened tonight between us. I see no point in discussing it further—with you or anyone else." She turned and walked up the steps to her front door. "And I hope you'll start reading your Bible."

She left him standing at the foot of the porch steps, staring after her with tears in his eyes.

The next morning, bright and early, Mrs. Greenwood was pounding on her door. Dorie had already left to visit the local newspaper and Ruth was having a second cup of tea.

"Good morning, Mrs. Greenwood," Ruth said as she opened the door.

Mrs. Greenwood rushed inside, bringing with her the icy chill of December. She was bundled in heavy scarf and mittens, and the tip of her nose and her round cheeks were red from the cold.

"Ruth," she said, peering at her with watery blue eyes, "I

just heard from Arthur that you've resigned from the clinic. Why did you do that? Don't you realize how much you are needed there?"

Ruth tried to suppress a deep sigh. "Mrs. Greenwood, would you like to come up for a cup of tea?" she asked in a voice that sounded more calm than she felt, in comparison to Mrs. Greenwood's breathless chatter.

"No, I haven't time. Why, Ruth? Why did you quit?"

Ruth sidestepped the question. "I'm not the only nurse in Dawson, Mrs. Greenwood. Arthur can get someone else to assist him at the clinic. Frankly, I'm worn out. We've worked long, tedious hours, and I really haven't had a chance to rest since losing my father."

Mrs. Greenwood tilted her head as she listened, thoughtfully taking in this bit of information.

"Well, yes. I know it's been difficult. But. . ." Her voice trailed as she seemed to have bogged down in her argument in Arthur's defense.

"Please don't concern yourself," Ruth said, her voice a bit firmer now. "I'm sure Dr. Bradley will manage without me."

A frown rumpled Mrs. Greenwood's brow as her watery blue eyes searched Ruth's face again. "He really cares for you, Ruth."

Ruth arched an eyebrow. "What does that have to do with my being a nurse?"

Mrs. Greenwood shifted from one foot to the other, and for a moment her eyes darted over the hallway. "I just wouldn't want to see Dr. Bradley get hurt. He's such a nice guy."

Ruth's mouth fell open. "What about my feelings, Mrs. Greenwood? Or is that not important? Are we only thinking of Dr. Bradley here?"

For a moment, Mrs. Greenwood was at a loss for words. Then she found her voice, and her tone was edged with anger.

"Mr. Greenwood and I feel it only fair to mention something, considering your father is no longer here to look out for you."

Ruth felt her back stiffen, and she knew they were about to get to the real purpose for Mrs. Greenwood's visit.

"That stranger you were with the other night—"

"His name is Joe Spencer, and he isn't a stranger to me. He visited the house when my father was alive; he even accompanied us to the midweek prayer service."

Mrs. Greenwood cleared her throat. "Well, the point is, he's collecting money on a claim that isn't even registered in his name."

Ruth gasped. "You mean you've already checked up on him?"

Mrs. Greenwood's face, already flushed from the cold, grew even redder. "Well, Mr. Greenwood was waiting for me at the door of the restaurant when I saw you two together. He said the next day he came in and collected money—quite a bit of it—on a claim that is registered to an Ivan Bertoff. He made no explanation of—"

"Did Mr. Greenwood inquire about this?" Ruth asked, unable to control her anger. She'd had quite enough of this woman's prattle, which extended beyond concern. She was being rude and critical of someone she knew nothing about.

"No, he—"

"Then perhaps I should remind you of what I told you during our Thanksgiving meal. Mr. Spencer has a partner in the claim, Ivan Bertoff. Since Mr. Greenwood has already checked, I'm sure he knows the claim is filed under Mr. Bertoff's name. Mr. Spencer takes care of the business end of their partnership. I see nothing sinister about that. If Mr. Bertoff has no objections, I can't see why anyone else should."

Mrs. Greenwood's eyebrows hiked at those words, and an ugly sneer contorted her features.

"Well, the way you are rushing to his defense obviously

betrays your feelings, Ruth. I'm shocked that you would take up with someone you know so little about. A miner, as compared to a man like Dr. Bradley."

"Mrs. Greenwood, I am not 'taking up,' as you put it, with anyone who is disreputable. Even so, I think I am the one to judge my friends, rather than you and Mr. Greenwood. I know you mean well, but I have begun to feel pressured to encourage Dr. Bradley's attention. I won't do that. While I respect his profession, I have no interest in him as a suitor. So maybe we can put that matter to rest, once and for all."

Mrs. Greenwood turned for the door. "In that case, I'll be leaving. You obviously resent my concern. I was mistaken to think you appreciated the fact that we cared about you, but I see that I have misjudged you. You are far too headstrong for your own good, young lady." Flinging that parting shot over her shoulder, she stormed out, slamming the door behind her.

Ruth glared at the door, seething with anger. She fought an urge to yank the door open and tell her if she cared about her, she should be checking on Arthur Bradley rather than Joe Spencer. At least she hadn't had to wrestle herself out of Joe's embrace, whereas Arthur had made a grab for her, practically forcing himself on her.

At the same time, she knew it would be unfair to speak her mind when she was angry, particularly after she had promised Arthur to say nothing of what had happened.

Turning, she rushed back up the stairs to the kitchen, trying to regain her composure. It took another cup of tea and a few minutes of introspection before she finally came to the conclusion that perhaps she had saved all of them time and trouble by stating her case. She did not want to be invited to any more of Mrs. Greenwood's dinners and have her trying to play Cupid. Furthermore, it would be a relief not to have the Greenwoods breathing down her neck. It was time someone let Mrs. Greenwood know that her busybody antics were not appreciated.

Despite her argument with herself, she was still feeling frustrated and listless when Dorie sailed in an hour later.

"I just met Kate Carmack!" Dorie said, grabbing a teacup and helping herself to tea. "Do you know her?"

Ruth was relieved to have a pleasant diversion from her conversation with Mrs. Greenwood.

"Yes. Her husband George and her brother Skookum Jim came to the clinic when we first opened. Both men were suffering from influenza."

"They're the ones who first discovered gold here, isn't that right?"

"So far as I know, yes, they were the first ones. Skookum Jim and Tagish Charlie are of the Tagish tribe, you know. They teamed up with George Carmack and discovered the first gold on Rabbit Creek. It's now called Bonanza Creek."

"I'm fascinated with Kate," Dorie said, propping her chin in her hand and staring into space.

"I want to do an article on her—the first woman in the Klondike gold fields. The people at home will be fascinated. What's even more interesting is her background. She was raised in the south central region here. She lost her first husband and their infant daughter, she told me."

"That's right," Ruth nodded. "They died of influenza, which is why she insisted on George and Skookum Jim seeing a doctor. Kate's a remarkable woman who kept the men in supplies by taking in laundry and sewing and selling moccasins to the miners. She also picked berries and set traps for rabbits. I've heard from several people that without her, her husband and brother could not have survived the first desperate winter here."

Dorie shook her head. "It's amazing what women will do for their men."

Ruth sipped her tea, thinking about that. Until Joe Spencer, she had never met anyone who would inspire her to take in laundry or sew or do any of the grueling tasks that were common to so many of the women whose husbands were miners. Still, when a woman really cared for a man, she could see that the tasks that seemed so difficult at least had purpose.

"I should add that it's also very amazing what doctors and nurses do for people," Dorie added, smiling across at Ruth. "I admire you so much, Ruth."

"Do you?" Ruth asked, surprised.

"Why, of course. You've shown real courage and stamina by coming here and then by treating all the sick people."

Ruth dropped her head, aware that she no longer had that purpose.

"Now what did I say wrong?" Dorie inquired, leaning forward.

Ruth began to tell her what had happened with Arthur Bradley and then Mrs. Greenwood.

"And you've let a narrow-minded person like that ruin your day?"

Ruth sighed. "The Greenwoods have been good to me." She went on to tell about the Sunday dinners and the fact that Mrs. Greenwood had come to the house when her father died, had held her in her arms as though she were her daughter.

"I'm already feeling guilty for what I said to her." Ruth frowned into her teacup, wishing she had not lost her temper.

"Well, a person can't go around poking their nose in other people's business and expect to be complimented for it. I'm sure you'll have a chance to make amends, if that's what you want. Tell me more about this Joe Spencer. You probably don't know it, but your eyes light up when you mention his name. I'd say you're smitten," she said, teasing her.

Ruth got up and went to the stove for the teakettle, needing the action to cover her sudden nervousness at Dorie's frank observation.

"He's a nice man. Mrs. Greenwood wants to insinuate that I should be wary of him, but I know she's trying to shove me into Arthur Bradley's arms."

"Hmmph. I would have difficulty dealing with someone who wanted to choose a man for me. If I wanted a man, I would choose one myself, which I did once." She sighed. "It didn't work out, which is one reason I jumped at the opportunity to come up here."

Ruth refilled Dorie's teacup and glanced at her new friend. For a moment, an expression of sadness crossed Dorie's face, and Ruth couldn't help wondering what went wrong with the man she had chosen, but she didn't ask. She knew, in time, if Dorie wanted to tell her, she would.

"I want you to know I'm so happy to have you living here," Ruth said to her. "Just being able to talk out my frustrations means a lot. You've made me feel a lot better."

"Good! Try not to worry over things that cannot be helped. My theory is just do your best and let God do the rest."

Ruth's smile widened. "That's a wonderful theory. I'll try to practice it more."

"Well," Dorie came to her feet, "now that I've enjoyed your good tea, I'm going to my room to do some writing while I'm still fired up about Kate Carmack."

"And I'll put something on the stove for lunch. Are you very hungry?"

"No, I'm not accustomed to eating a lot. So just yell whenever you want me to come help."

"Thanks," Ruth said, quietly thanking God for sending Dorie to her.

☙

Two days later, a handsome man dressed in parka and jeans

appeared at her door. He had brown hair, deep thoughtful eyes, and an engaging smile. "Are you Miss Wright?" he asked politely.

"Yes, I am," she replied, studying him curiously.

"Hi, I'm Jack London," he said. "I have a little cabin near Joe and Ivan. When Joe heard I was coming into town for supplies, he asked me to drop this off to you."

He handed her a sheet of paper, folded into a neat square, with her name on it.

"Thank you," she said, accepting the note. She looked back at the man, who was regarding her with curious yet friendly eyes.

"How is Joe?" she asked.

"He's working very hard, but generally he seems to be okay." He smiled briefly. "Well, I must go. It was nice meeting you."

"You, too," she replied then stepped back inside. She hurried up to her bedroom and sat down to read the note, written in bold yet neat handwriting.

*Dear Ruth,*

*I wanted to thank you for a wonderful evening. Also, I want you to know how much I appreciate the invitation to Christmas dinner. I will look very forward to sharing that special day with you as I battle the cold and the drudgery that is my life here. I have not looked forward to Christmas very much for several years. This year is different. I can hardly wait to see you again and enjoy the pleasure of your company.*

*Until then, take very good care of yourself.*

*Your friend,*
*Joe*

She smiled, traced a finger over the paper, and tried to imagine him sitting down in the small cabin he had described to her, thoughtfully writing out the letter. She sighed, pressing the letter against her heart.

*Thank you, God*, she silently prayed. How could Mrs. Greenwood or anyone doubt the sincerity of this wonderful man?

Singing a Christmas carol, she got up and went to her room, wondering what she would wear when he came to see her.

## nine

As the Christmas season approached, some of the merchants made noble attempts to honor the birth of Christ. Wreaths and candles dominated the shop windows and a few of the log homes. However, it was common knowledge to all that there would be no bountiful feasts on anyone's table on Christmas Day, for now even the merchants were worrying about what they would eat. Many of the staples on which people depended were completely gone from the shelves, except for the few hidden away for the merchants and their families. Most people would gladly have paid the asking price of a dollar per orange back in the fall, but now there were no oranges or fruit of any kind, except for the dried variety.

Ruth tried to keep her spirits up, despite the absence of so many things. She had spent many hours with her needle and thread, making little white angels from used white petticoats, using buttons for eyes and making hair from yarn. Noticing the angels, one of the merchants had begged her to make more to sell in shops, but Ruth was out of yarn and buttons, and couldn't make more without cutting up clothes, and she didn't want to do that. The red silk petticoat she had brought to Dawson had seemed absurdly out of place once she arrived. Now, however, it was about to serve a purpose. Working adeptly with scissors, needle, and thread, she cut and shaped it into a tablecloth for the holidays while thinking of the meal she would prepare for Joe Spencer. During the drab season, the reminder that he was eating Christmas dinner with her kept her going when she might have been moping like so many others.

Lucky, her father's devoted patient, had brought a small spruce tree to her for a Christmas present; and in return, she had gone through her father's medicine cabinet, selecting liniments and cough syrups for Lucky.

She had sewn a few ornaments for the tree and strung popcorn and holly for decorations. She removed one branch, already decorated, from the back side of the tree and took it to the cemetery. There, she thrust it into the hard-packed snow as a tribute to her father for the happy Christmases they had shared.

Two days before Christmas, she braved the subzero weather by bundling up in her warmest clothes, wearing three pair of socks, and her sturdiest rubber boots to make a trek through the snow to the mercantile.

She was half-frozen by the time she arrived. Opening the door and expecting to be warmed by the potbellied stove inside, she was surprised to see the clerks bundled up in coats and mittens and the patrons huddling as close as possible to the stove. Although the store was warmer than outside, it was a startling contrast to the once-cozy, warm store of two weeks before.

As she approached the clerk, he greeted her and offered an apology. "We are having to ration our wood," he said, nodding toward the stove. "I apologize. Why don't you warm yourself while I get your items for you, Miss Wright?"

"Thank you." Shivering from the cold, she glanced at the stove, grateful for the supply of wood her father had accumulated. She removed her mittens and with stiff fingers opened her string purse and removed the list.

The clerk hurried off with the list. Ruth felt as though her legs had become wooden posts as she edged toward the stove where everyone huddled.

"Miss Wright," a familiar voice called to her.

She turned to see Arthur Bradley. Noting the *Miss Wright*, she appreciated the fact that he was being more formal now that she had broken her friendship with him.

"Hello," she said, trying to move her cold lips into a smile.

"I'm sorry to see you out in the cold," he said, looking concerned. He had lost more weight and was now pitifully thin. His cheeks were gaunt and there were dark circles under his eyes.

"I needed the fresh air. Are you well?" she asked, looking him over with concern.

"Not very, but I will manage."

"What's wrong?" she asked worriedly, for she did care about him as a friend, after all.

He shrugged. "Just a bout of influenza that I was able to conquer. I have worried about you," he added, his pale green eyes staring into her face.

"I have taken in a boarder," she said on a more cheerful note. "A nice lady named Dorie Farmer. She is a correspondent for the San Francisco *Examiner*."

He did not react with the relief she would have expected, and then she realized why. He wanted to be the one she turned to for help. He didn't want her to survive on her own without him.

"I hope the arrangement is working out," he said, his voice as doubtful as Mrs. Greenwood's had been.

Remembering their argument, Ruth lifted her chin and took on a more firm stance. "The arrangement is working out just fine, thank you."

"Here are the items you needed, Miss Wright."

To her relief, the clerk had returned with two large bundles, heavily wrapped. "We are out of coffee, sugar, and salt." He pointed to the list. "I'm sorry."

She turned to the clerk, hovering nearby, looking distressed. "But. . ." Her voice trailed as she glanced at the men knotted around the stove. Her father had said the merchants would retain a stash of items for themselves and the doctors.

But her father was dead and she was no longer a nurse, she reminded herself.

"Maybe I can help you." Arthur lowered his voice.

Pride surged back as she looked from the clerk to Arthur. "Thank you, but I can manage just fine. I have enough in my pantry to make do." She turned and followed the clerk to the counter, opening her string purse to pay for her purchases. To her surprise, it took almost all of the money she had.

After she had paid, Arthur trailed her to the door, opening it for her. "Won't you join me at the Greenwoods' home for Christmas dinner?" he asked suddenly.

"I have made plans for Christmas," she answered as they stepped out onto the snow-covered boards. When she looked at him, she saw the pain on his face. She felt desperately sorry to have hurt him and wished she could make amends. "Arthur, I want you to understand that I am no longer upset with you. I have forgotten our. . .differences."

"Then what is it?" he asked miserably.

She hesitated for a moment as she pulled her scarf over her head and about her face, tucking it into her collar. She decided she might as well be honest with him. "I have met someone," she answered.

His pale brows arched suddenly. "Are you talking about that drifter?"

"I don't know to whom you are referring, but I can assure you I haven't taken up with a drifter, Arthur."

He frowned, obviously trying to remember a name. Then his eyes snapped as though something had dawned on him. "The miner, Spencer, whom no one knows anything about."

She sighed. "I see you and Mrs. Greenwood have been talking. Well, I can assure you that Mr. Spencer is a gentleman.

Furthermore, Dorie will be joining us, so it isn't as though we will be unchaperoned. Merry Christmas, Arthur."

She turned and left him staring after her on the snowy boards in front of the mercantile. As she hurried home, gripping her packages tightly against her chest for warmth, anger churned through her, warming her and quickening her steps. By the time she reached the porch steps, gripping the post as she raked the caked snow from her boots, her temper was boiling.

She was sick and tired of Arthur and the Greenwoods trying to run her life. They seemed determined to conspire in an arranged marriage between Arthur and her, which made her more determined than ever to avoid them. Furthermore, she thought with a smile, it made Joe Spencer even more appealing.

❧

On Christmas Day, she and Dorie were in the kitchen early. While she, too, had been forced to ration her wood, the kitchen was warm and cozy. Dorie had volunteered to make a berry pie from some huckleberries she had been hoarding in a leather pouch since early fall.

"I kept these against starvation on Chilkoot Pass then forgot about them until I unpacked my belongings. I will make us a berry pie."

"Can you stretch the sugar?" Ruth teased.

"That I can do," Dorie laughed as they worked side by side, putting together the meal.

Lucky had brought a duck to Ruth in late fall, and she had wrapped it in a thickness of cheesecloth and buried it in the snow to freeze it. Two days ago, she had retrieved it, thawed it on the stove, and last night she had put it in to bake.

"We may be the only people in Dawson who are having meat for our meal," Dorie said, suddenly looking sad. "Some of my friends at the *Nugget* were complaining that their Christmas meal would be drastically different this year.

Unless one is a hunter willing to brave the elements, there is no meat left in Dawson, I hear."

Ruth nodded. "God has been good to us."

"And you certainly know how to conserve your food supply. I've been amazed at the way you do that."

Ruth laughed as she placed the bread on its baking pan. "I had a very comfortable upbringing in Seattle, and yet my mother came from a family with nine children. She was always very practical in the kitchen, and I learned many tricks from her."

Dorie smiled. "I've watched you pick up half a leftover biscuit and dump it in that tin." She nodded toward the large tin that was a familiar object in Ruth's kitchen.

"And now I have enough corn bread and biscuit to put together my dressing for today," Ruth said, feeling a bit of satisfaction at how she was managing her supplies.

"So I see," Dorie laughed. "And what time is our guest arriving?"

Automatically, Ruth's eyes drifted toward the kitchen window. "I should think any time now."

Then she glanced down at her dress. Beneath the muslin apron, she wore her green woolen dress, and she had styled her hair in a softer chignon today. Deep waves on the sides of her face softened her eyes, and she knew the happiness along with the heat of the oven would color her lips and cheeks.

Almost as soon as Dorie had posed the question of their guest, she heard the neigh of a horse.

She clapped her hands together, dusting off the loose flour. Picking up a cup towel, she wiped her fingers as she walked to the window and peered out.

Joe had arrived and was steering his horse toward the hitching post. He was carrying a bundle of something in a tote sack in his arms, while one gloved hand gripped the reins.

Balancing the load, he dismounted his horse. Both man and horse were covered with snow. He wore a heavy parka with hood, and his face was red with cold. Before he could look up and catch her gawking, she quickly stepped back from the window.

"He's here," she said and beamed across at Dorie.

"So I gathered," Dorie chuckled. "Look, you've done everything other than bake the bread. Why don't you let me finish up the meal while you visit with him in the living room?"

Ruth hesitated then quickly consented. "If you don't mind," she said, hurrying from the kitchen.

She left the door open to admit more heat into the living room. Removing her apron and laying it over the back of a chair, she began to punch up the goose down feathers on the sofa. She moved to the bookcase, straightening a few toppled books and wiping a fleck of dust away. Then she turned back to her tree, staring at it for a moment with pride.

In spite of her meager circumstances, she had managed to obtain a cheerful mood both in her home and within herself. She had spent a few hours crying over the fact that her father would not be sharing Christmas with them, but then she had counted her blessings of Dorie and Joe, which always lifted her spirits.

As soon as she heard his knock on the door, she rushed down the stairs into the cold hall and quickly opened the door.

He looked taller and leaner than ever, and this time he had grown a blond-brown beard, neatly trimmed. The blue eyes looked even larger in his bronze face, and she realized that he had indeed lost weight. Her eyes ran down his lean body and she saw, from the horsehair mat, that he had done his best to remove the snow from his shoes.

"Hello." She smiled at him.

"Merry Christmas," he said, still holding the mysterious bundle. "I've brought along some firewood that I thought you might use."

"Wonderful," she said with delight, for wood was a major problem for everyone in Dawson. "I can't tell you how much I appreciate that. Why don't you just put it down here in the hall by the coat tree?"

He entered the hall, placing the sack on the floor with a thud. Then carefully he began to remove his snow-dusted parka. From the pocket he retrieved a small package, and Ruth hoped it was not a gift for she had nothing for him. He turned to face her, looking more handsome than ever in his white dress shirt and dark trousers.

"Was it rough traveling over the road?"

"Not too bad," he replied, his eyes barely leaving hers. "This is for you," he said, extending the small brown-wrapped package to her.

She swallowed, feeling embarrassed. "I. . .I have nothing for you."

He had closed the door, but still the frigid air that had rushed in surrounded them.

"I beg to differ. You have given me one of the best gifts I've ever received—the joy of your company on Christmas Day."

Her eyes locked with his for a moment, and she finally admitted to herself what she had secretly known all along. She was in love with Joe Spencer.

The bump of something overhead shook her back to her senses. "Please come upstairs," she said, smiling into his deep blue eyes.

"I'll remove my boots and leave them here by the door," he said, preparing to remove the heavy work boots.

Upon removing his boots, she saw that he had also brought

along an extra pair of clean leather boots, and he was putting those on now. *What a kind, considerate man he is,* she thought as her heart beat faster.

Turning for the stairs, she lifted her skirts and walked ahead of him, holding his present as though it were a precious treasure, which it was. When they entered the living room, she saw that Dorie had emerged from the kitchen and stood eagerly waiting to meet Joe. As Joe and Dorie faced one another for the first time, Dorie's eyes widened for a moment and she tilted her head thoughtfully.

As Ruth made the introductions and both responded, Dorie retained that same thoughtful expression. "I have the feeling we've met before, Mr. Spencer," she said, eyeing him up and down.

He stroked his whiskered chin. "I'm sure I would have remembered, Miss Farmer," he said in his smooth southern drawl.

"Dorie is a correspondent for the San Francisco *Examiner.*"

"I see," he said, shifting his eyes back to Ruth. "Then it's possible we may have passed one another on a street in San Francisco," he said.

Ruth thought he seemed to be explaining the fact more to Ruth than Dorie, so she turned back for Dorie's reaction.

"Yes, that's possible," Dorie nodded. "Anyway, being a journalist, I don't usually forget a face. Particularly a handsome one," she added boldly.

Ruth laughed and Joe joined in rather self-consciously. "Thank you. Nor am I inclined to forget a pretty woman like yourself."

Dorie ducked her head and blushed, obviously unaccustomed to such a compliment. Ruth smiled at Joe, knowing he was being kind. Dorie was many wonderful things, but pretty was not an adjective she would use to describe her.

"How can I help in the preparations?" he asked as Ruth went to put his package under the tree.

"If you'd like to wash up in the kitchen, I'll give you a job," she said. She had decided to let him join in the preparations so that he would feel more like he had a part in their celebration. "I haven't had time to sweep the hall steps or the hall. If you wouldn't mind the task, I'll give that to you while Dorie and I finish with the meal."

"I'll be happy to do that," he said, accepting the homemade broom Dorie handed him.

When the two women were alone in the kitchen, Dorie rolled her eyes. "You didn't tell me he was so good-looking or so charming."

"I'm keeping that secret to myself," Ruth teased back.

While their meal was scant if compared to the other Christmas dinners Ruth had enjoyed throughout her life, Dorie and Joe complimented her and she, too, enjoyed the food. Afterwards, they settled down around the tree to open presents.

At Ruth's suggestion, Dorie opened her present first. Ruth had made a cloth cover for the journal that Dorie carried everywhere. When Dorie opened it, she was ecstatic.

"I'm so grateful that my journal will be protected from the elements," she said, beaming proudly. "Thank you, Ruth. Now you open yours."

Dorie had given Ruth a collection of recipes that she had organized into a neat little book. Ruth was delighted.

"The recipes came from the Tlingit woman who accompanied her husband, guiding us over the Chilkoot. She was our cook, and I found some of her native dishes quite wonderful. Also, she had a very ingenuous way of preparing things. I copied down her methods, but not being a cook, I doubt that I will ever have use for them." She laughed self-consciously as she looked at Joe, who smiled back at her.

"Thank you so much, Dorie," Ruth replied. "How thoughtful of you."

The remaining gift to be opened was from Joe, and Ruth hesitated. She had thought it improper to buy a gift for Joe, and now she felt a bit awkward in accepting one from him.

"The gift is merely an acknowledgment of your kindness and that of your father," he added. "They treated me with a back injury," he explained to Dorie, "and I felt Doc never charged enough for his services."

Ruth smiled, grateful that he could explain away any improprieties of the gift. When she opened the paper, she found, wrapped in delicate tissue, a small pin fashioned from a gold nugget.

She gasped, holding the tiny gleaming gold in the palm of her hand. "This is gorgeous."

Joe smiled, looking pleased that she liked his gift. "We are doing fairly well with our claim. The last time I was in Dawson, I stopped in at Mr. Bromberg's little house, having heard he had been a jeweler in New York. He agreed to design the pin for me, and he did it rather quickly."

"But. . . ," Ruth looked from Dorie to Joe, "I can't accept anything this expensive. What about. . ." She had been about to suggest he send it to his mother, but she was dead. "Do you have any sisters?"

Joe shook his head. "No, I don't. You really shouldn't be self-conscious about it. I've explained my motives. This is just a meager show of appreciation for what you and your father did for me."

"He's right," Dorie jumped in, eager to encourage Ruth. "There's no reason you shouldn't keep such a thoughtful gift." She looked at Joe. "You must be one of the few who is doing well with your claim."

"I suppose I am," he answered. As he spoke, Ruth thought his words held just a hint of formality. "I have a partner, Ivan Bertoff, a Russian gentleman who originally filed the claim. I think I've been lucky to join up with him."

Ruth sighed deeply, then covered the sigh with a smile when both Dorie and Joe looked at her. After Mrs. Greenwood and Arthur's badgering, it was wonderful to hear the truth about his claim spoken in the presence of Dorie, who was sure to back her up or even spread the word herself.

"I'm happy for you." She was staring at him again, and both Ruth and Joe noticed. "I still have the odd feeling we have met. When did you arrive in the territory?"

There was a moment's hesitation. "The boat pulled into Dawson the first of August. I'm originally from San Francisco, but we already agreed that we must have passed one another in a shop somewhere and not realized it until now."

Dorie nodded, apparently satisfied by the answer. "I'm rather nondescript, let's face facts. So it's quite possible you wouldn't remember me. Well," she said, looking from Joe to Ruth, "I did promise the Fairhopes that I would drop in on them this afternoon for tea and spice cake."

She came to her feet, clutching Ruth's gift to her chest. "It has been a wonderful Christmas."

Joe stood, then Ruth did, as well. For a moment, she felt a bit awkward. She hoped Dorie wasn't inventing an excuse for her to be alone with Joe. She opened her mouth to say something, but there seemed to be no adequate response. She had no doubt the Fairhopes had invited Dorie for tea. Since the Fairhopes owned the local newspaper, it was quite logical they would invite Dorie to drop by on Christmas Day.

"I've enjoyed spending part of the day with you," Joe said to her.

"Thank you." That self-conscious look that often slipped over Dorie's face in Joe's presence returned as she hurried into her bedroom and began to rummage around.

"I believe I'll go down and bring up some of that firewood," he said, turning for the door.

"I'll help," Ruth offered.

"It isn't necessary," Dorie called back, already busy in the kitchen.

For the brief time she was alone in the living room, she admired her pin again. Then, to show her appreciation, she decided to wear it. She fastened the delicate clasp at the neck of her dress, and the little pin gleamed brilliantly against her white collar. She was literally soaring with joy over the wonderful day they had spent together. Thinking back, it was one of the finest Christmas Days ever.

Dorie entered the room again, a box in her hand. "I save all of my newspaper articles," she said, indicating the box. "I hope that doesn't seem too vain, but I thought I'd take over some of the articles I wrote about Skagway. Mr. Fairhope thought we might be able to use something in the paper here, since everyone is hungry for news of other areas, how they've done with gold mining, that sort of thing. Skagway had a rough time surviving last year, so perhaps seeing how those courageous people made do just may help the people here."

Joe's footsteps sounded on the stairs, and Dorie glanced toward the open door.

"He brought firewood," Ruth explained, smiling.

"He's a gift from above." The words formed on Dorie's lips, though she did not voice them for Joe was entering the living room. He glanced at Dorie, who stood with her cloak on, preparing to leave. "I'll just stoke up your fire in the stove," he said to Ruth.

"Good day, Mr. Spencer. I'll be out for a while. I trust you'll be here when I return and join us at the Christmas service?"

A look of regret crossed his face. "I have to leave to return to the mine today. It will be getting dark soon. Will you be all right alone?" he asked with concern, looking at Dorie.

"The Fairhopes will see me home, thank you."

There was only four hours of daylight now, and Ruth had begun to dread the darkness that seemed so interminable. She knew it was a long journey for him, and yet she wished he could stay.

"You aren't staying at Miss Mattie's this time?" she asked, trying to keep a cheerful note to her voice.

"No. With the bad weather, we're very limited on our working hours. We have to take advantage of the short daylight and the fact that there's no more snow right now."

"But how do you work with so much snow?"

"We just have to keep fires going, dig, and windlass, but we are very limited in that and can only do so during the middle of the day, when the temperature is not as brutal."

"But it's still brutal, isn't it?" she asked, following him to the kitchen and watching as he put more wood into the stove. "I walked to the mercantile a few days ago and it was agony. I really don't see how you do it."

He finished with the fire, closed the stove door, and wiped his hands on the old towel she handed him. "Ambition, I guess. And truthfully, I enjoy mining."

"Do you?" she asked, surprised to hear that. "So many consider it a drudgery and are in it only with the hope of getting rich quick."

He grinned as they walked back to the living room. "Well, that's part of the reason I enjoy it, I suppose."

As they took their seats, Ruth studied his face, noting he was the only man with a beard whom she regarded as handsome. It seemed despite good barbers and conveniences of the city, Joe always managed to look good. His shoulder-length hair and thick beard, though neatly trimmed, did not make him less appealing to her.

"You've asked if I plan to stay on in Dawson. What are your plans?" She had been so curious about him, wanting to know everything, yet reluctant to ask.

"I want to return to San Francisco," he said matter-of-factly.

"You do?" She was surprised by the answer, even though she knew she shouldn't be. He had lived in San Francisco before.

He nodded, looking across at the little Christmas tree. "I enjoyed ranch life and have ridiculous aspirations of someday owning a ranch." He turned back to her with a grin. "I suppose it's the love of land in my blood from generations of plantation owners. When my ancestors lost their land after the Civil War, they were never quite the same, or so I've been told. Anyway, there must be that need to own my own spot of ground." He paused, looking toward the window where darkness was already beginning to gather. "If I can't buy a small ranch, I hope to at least homestead a few acres and build a cabin. I think Ivan and I will make enough money for that."

She nodded, thinking of what he was saying. "That's a realistic dream." And it was his dream that turned her thoughts back to her own future. She had been worried sick about what she was going to do. She could sell the house here and the funds would sustain her for a while back in Seattle, but then what? She still had the house there, but it would need repairs, and there were her future needs to consider. She was trained for nursing, but now that held no appeal, either. What she really wanted was a husband and a family. She hadn't realized she was staring at Joe until he spoke.

"Is something wrong?" he asked gently. "Food in my beard?" he teased.

She flushed and laughed softly. "I'm sorry. I was miles away, thinking of my future."

"And what is your future, may I ask?"

She shook her head. "I'm not sure. Since I can't depend on a bonanza from mining—" She broke off, suddenly remembering the claim her father had taken from a patient. It was tucked away in a bureau drawer; in fact, she had almost forgotten about it. Automatically, her eyes drifted toward her bedroom as her mind seized upon a plan. If Joe knew mining, was willing to work so hard to succeed at it, perhaps he was the person to consult. Of course he was!

"Excuse me for a moment," she said, getting up and hurrying into the bedroom. Opening the middle drawer of her chest, she moved aside a layer of undergarments and retrieved the piece of paper that neither she nor even her father had taken very seriously.

Gripping it in her hands, glancing over it, she walked back into the living room. "Would you please take a look at this?"

His brows lifted as she handed the paper to him. He scanned it then looked at her in surprise. "It's a claim that's located not far from ours. I believe that should be a good area."

Ruth smiled, pleased with that news. "A miner with tuberculosis gave it to my father in payment for treating him for a week before he departed, saying he never wanted to see this area again. He was a very sick man, and my father gave him money for boat passage back to the States. That's when he gave us the claim."

She went back to her seat. "I don't think my father thought much of it. He had probably even forgotten about it when you asked if he had any aspirations to be a miner. He had heard so many stories of men about to strike it rich, only to watch them come back empty-handed and terribly ill."

She touched the gold nugget at her neck. "You obviously

know what you're doing. Would you be interested in taking me on as a partner?"

He stared at her for a moment as though he couldn't believe what she had asked. Then his eyes dropped to the claim, and he read it again. "I don't know what to say," he finally replied. "I would be honored to be your partner. And I will do my best with this." He indicated the paper. "Are you sure there isn't anyone else you want to do business with?"

She laughed. "Not unless Clarence Berry is interested, and I believe he is currently enjoying his wealth in another area." Her laughter died away as she looked at him seriously. "No one else has brought me firewood, or a present on Christmas Day, or been the gentleman that you have been. I'm certain that you're the one I want to entrust my claim to, although it may be worthless. I don't want to waste your time."

Joe stared at the claim again. The location was prime, although these things were always a gamble. The emotion he had felt for Ruth was brimming up inside him now. If she were that honest with him, how could he be less with her? He had to tell her about the incident in Skagway.

He drew a deep breath, wondering how to begin.

"Why don't I make us some coffee?" she suggested.

He shook his head. "I'm learning to enjoy plain tea."

"Good. I have more tea than coffee. There's very little coffee left, and Dorie and I limit ourselves to half a cup of very weak coffee each morning in order to wake up."

"And I'll not deprive you of that," he said, standing. "I'll join you in the kitchen."

As he walked behind her, his eyes roamed over her shining auburn hair, the straight back and tiny waist, the slim hips in her flowing skirt. He had to tell her, he had to. *But how?* How could he make her understand? And if she knew, it would be her duty to contact the Mounties. Would she do that? He suspected that she would not; on the other hand, she wouldn't go through with their partnership on the mining claim.

Looking down, his mind weighed the alternatives. If she were willing to trust him with the claim, he might be the only one who would deal honestly with her. And if the claim made them rich, he could go back to Skagway, hire a decent attorney, face the truth. Or he could get on the boat with her and return to the States. Given those choices, he could not bring himself to be honest enough, or reckless enough, to throw away a bright future.

By the time they took their seats at the table and sipped tea, he had carefully folded the claim and put it in his breast pocket, buttoning down the flap.

"I promise you I will work hard on this claim—"

"It isn't necessary to make any promises. You've proven you are a hard worker. Just don't make yourself ill like the last man who owned it. And really, Joe, I have nothing to lose. That claim has just been occupying space in the drawer. When I leave next spring, I doubt that I would be able to get a fair price for it." She sighed. "I've heard how people take advantage of widows with mining claims, and in some ways I'm very much like those widows."

He reached across, covering her soft hand with his. "But you are not a widow. And to my enormous good fortune, you are not betrothed."

He looked into her eyes and felt his love for her filling every corner of his heart. Maybe he couldn't tell her about Skagway just yet, but he could share his feelings for her and he would be honest in what he said.

"Ruth, this has been the most special Christmas of my life."

She gasped, and her eyes widened. "Surely as a boy with your family—"

"No." He shook his head. "I was not with the woman I loved. And I do love you, Ruth."

As her cheeks colored at those words, he rushed on. "I want you to know I'm not speaking impulsively or dishonestly. I've had many long nights to think about this, to think of you and nothing else. Please forgive me if I'm being too forward. I don't want to embarrass or offend you."

Her eyes were glowing as she squeezed his hand, and he breathed a sigh of relief as she answered him. "Your words neither embarrass nor offend me. I am filled with joy that you feel this way because. . ." She faltered, dropped her eyes to their clasped hands for a moment. Then, as though she had gathered her courage, she lifted her hazel eyes to him and spoke in a firm voice. "Because I feel the same way. I love you, too, Joe."

His breath caught. A joy too sweet to believe filled his being. He had never in his life felt such happiness, such hope. He stood, lifting her hand to his chest, drawing her gently from her chair.

"I love you," he repeated, his hands cupping the sides of her heart-shaped face as he kissed her with all the fervor of a man deeply in love. She returned his kiss, and as their lips expressed their joy, she pulled back from him, breathlessly. The light flushed her cheeks and the radiance in her eyes told him she would be a wonderful wife, eager to accept his affections and return them. She would not be cold or impassive, as he had heard some men complain.

"Ruth, would you—" He stopped himself. How could he propose to her without telling her everything? And if he did, he would lose her.

Her face was tilted slightly, and she seemed to be holding her breath, waiting.

"I don't want to rush you," he said, gently backing himself

out of the situation. "I just want you to be certain about how you feel. We'll talk more seriously when I return."

At that, he glanced over his shoulder and saw complete darkness through the window. He sighed, releasing her. "I have to go."

"I don't want you to," she said suddenly then bit her lip. "But of course you must. I hear of accidents on the trail, and there is always the danger of frostbite from exposure. Please be careful." Her voice was low and plaintive, drawing him back to her.

He kissed her again, quickly this time, and then he forced himself to head for the door. He knew that with each minute he spent with her, the opportunity to leave was becoming more difficult. He longed to stay with her. . .forever. But he must earn her love and their future, and that meant returning to the freezing, torturous work that lay ahead of him.

She followed him down the stairs, crossing her arms over her chest, watching silently as he removed his boots and pulled on the heavier ones, then bundled himself back into the parka.

"Could I give you an extra blanket?" she asked suddenly.

"I carry one in my saddlebag," he said. "Merry Christmas, Ruth." He hesitated at the doorway, again hating to leave.

"Merry Christmas, Joe." This time it was she who leaned forward and brushed his lips with a kiss.

The kiss warmed his lips against the freezing night that enveloped him, and the memory of the glow in her eyes, the words she had spoken—*she loved him!*—gave him the endurance he needed to return through the bleak winter night to the drafty cabin he shared with Ivan.

# ten

The cold darkness of January seemed interminable. Only a few hours of daylight broke the monotony, and during those hours Ruth and Dorie tried to maintain their chores. Dorie worked long hours at the newspaper office, for the small newspaper was a major source of entertainment for the residents of Dawson.

Ruth spent much of her time planning the best way to convert their dwindling supply of food into nutritional meals. More and more she turned to God for strength. She read her mother's Bible often, and many days she was tempted to sink into grief. It was the memory of Joe Spencer, however, that always gave her hope and joy.

She had not heard from him since Christmas Day, when he left the house. They had been enveloped in a glow of love that day, a glow that warmed her during the fiercely cold nights when the wind howled around the eaves of her house. Then she longed for Joe's strong arms, and she worried that he was cold or hungry or sick. When worry burdened her heart, she prayed. Many nights, the wee hours found her on her knees by her bed, a blanket wrapped around her shoulders to warm her as she asked God to protect her beloved. She had lost both parents, and now she agonized about losing Joe.

During the first week of February, a heavily bundled Arthur Bradley appeared at her door, hugging a sack against his chest. Although surprised to see him, Ruth found herself glad that he had come, and she quickly invited him inside, for there was only a thin sliver of daylight and it was freezing cold outside.

147

"Ruth, I have more food than I need," he said, following her up the stairs to the living area. "I wanted to share a few items with you. I've been worrying about you."

"I'm fine, Arthur," she answered with a smile.

He waved aside her reply as they entered the kitchen and he placed the sack on the counter. "I'm sure you are. However, with very little daylight and the weather so terribly cold, I don't like the thought of you trying to walk to the mercantile. And if you did," he said, shaking his head, "you wouldn't find much to purchase."

She sighed. "It's really bad, isn't it?"

He was removing his parka, his scarf, and then his gloves. "Yes, I'm afraid the lack of food is getting quite serious. However, everyone seems to be making do, although I can tell you the faces are getting thinner and thinner."

She shook her head, turning for the stove. "Then let's have a cup of hot tea and be grateful for our blessings."

"A splendid idea," he said, taking a seat at the table.

When she asked about his work, he began to relate stories from the clinic. As they sat at the kitchen table sipping weak tea and discussing medicine, she felt relieved that he had come. In an odd way, it brought back conversations with her father. She had missed Arthur. When finally he lapsed into silence and looked deeply into her eyes, Ruth sensed that he still cared for her.

She got up to refill their teacups, wanting to escape the look of sadness in his eyes.

"Arthur, Dorie told me there is word of a missionary hospital to be established here later in the year. Is this true?" she asked, eager to divert his thoughts.

He blinked, as though clearing his head, and nodded. "Yes, I expect there will be a hospital, although it will be small and sparsely furnished in the beginning. Still, it is much needed, and I will not feel so guilty when I leave."

She sat down in the chair and looked across at him. "You are leaving, then?"

He nodded, staring at his cup. "As soon as I can. Of course, I will wait until some of the medical missionaries arrive, but I hope they will be on the first boat this spring. I hate it here, Ruth." He sighed. "I am not cut out for this type of life."

"Is anyone?" She smiled sadly.

"It doesn't seem to have bothered you as badly as most."

She considered the thought and shrugged. "Perhaps it is because I know there is nothing I can do to change my circumstances during this time. I just have to try and be patient."

"Patient for what?" he asked, frowning. "For travel to commence again so you can go home?"

She hesitated. For a moment, she longed to tell him about Joe, but then she knew it would only hurt him. She could no longer speak to him as a friend, for his feelings for her exceeded friendship, and she regretted that.

Noticing her hesitation, he continued. "Are you still seeing Mr. Spencer?"

"Yes," she replied and smiled in spite of herself. "I care for him, Arthur. And he cares for me. I don't know what the future holds, but I am happy for now."

"I see," he said, speaking more formally. "What news did he bring of his claim last week? Mr. Greenwood says he is the only miner making money. Maybe you didn't do so badly in choosing him," he said with a wry grin, "although it pains me to say so."

She stared at him, her mind closing over the other words he had spoken. "Last week?" she repeated, still wondering if she had heard him correctly. "You saw him last week?"

"Actually, I didn't. Mrs. Greenwood just remarked that her husband had measured out nuggets from one of Spencer's claims, and that the nuggets were quite promising. Perhaps he has struck a bonanza after all, although I'm sure it will be months before he can work in earnest, considering the weather conditions."

She heard the wind rattling a loose board at the corner of the house, and at the same time, something cold crept through her heart. If Joe had been in town, why hadn't he come to see her?

She lifted her teacup and took a sip, oblivious to the weak taste, to whatever else Arthur was saying. Why would Joe come to town and not visit her? She tried to ignore the sting of hurt, rationalizing that he might have come and knocked; perhaps she had been in the back of the house and not heard him. So often the boards rattled and she had learned to ignore the occasional bump. If she had not been looking out the window as Arthur arrived, she might not have gone to the door.

Arthur took out his pocket watch and sighed. "Amazing how the hours drag during the lonely darkness. I've spent an hour here with you, and yet it seems that only a few minutes have passed."

Ruth forced a smile as she put down her teacup. "I hope you aren't working too hard," she said, her voice sounding odd in her own ears.

"I am, but I prefer to stay busy. Frostbite is rampant. And scurvy. Miss Mattie's boardinghouse is full. Many of the miners have given up and come in for the duration of the winter. It was a wise decision. Some would have died, otherwise." He stood. "Thank you for your hospitality. You have brightened my day."

"Thank you for coming, Arthur." She glanced at the items on the kitchen counter that he had brought to her.

"You were kind to bring food. Dorie will be appreciative, too. Have you met her?"

He nodded, looking pleased. "I am so relieved that she is

living with you, Ruth. She seems like a nice woman, and I don't think you need to be here alone," he said, his eyes trailing over the kitchen.

"She's an answer to prayer. It has proven to be a most satisfactory arrangement for both of us," she said, following him back through the living room. She hugged her arms around her, almost hating to see him go. She thought of the night he had kissed her and the anger she had felt. All that was in the past now. He was still concerned for her, despite her rebuking him, concerned enough to bring food.

Why hadn't Joe done that?

She followed him down to the front door, bracing herself for the icy blast of cold that would hit her once the door was opened.

"Good-bye, Arthur. Take care," she said, watching him as he huddled into his parka and drew the woolen scarf about his chin.

"You, too," he said, his words muffled by the scarf.

"Good-bye," she said, closing the door. The cold quickly penetrated her woolen dress, following her as she hurried back upstairs. She wondered why people didn't drop dead in the streets. To live in Dawson, one had to be a survivor; lack of knowledge could take a life in minutes. Most people knew exactly how long it would take for exposed skin to freeze. They also knew it was committing suicide to try and challenge the elements. As she hurried back to the warmth of the kitchen, she thought about what the past year had brought to her.

Never a patient person, she had learned patience, and she had learned to trust God. She had no choice. It was comforting to know that God was watching over her. Even today. He had sent Arthur with food when she had prayed yesterday for knowledge of how to best stretch the meager items left in her pantry.

She opened the sack and examined the tinned goods. . .and the small pouch of coffee.

"Oh, Arthur," she sighed, lifting the pouch and relishing the smell of coffee beans. It had been weeks since she and Dorie had tasted coffee. Now they were in for a treat.

*Joe*, she thought miserably, *why didn't you come? Why didn't you bring me coffee and food?*

Closing her eyes and pressing the leather pouch against her cheek, she tried to fight off the tears that welled in her eyes.

"You came," she spoke into the silence of the kitchen. "I know you came to my door and I didn't hear you. And the door was locked. Oh, Joe, I'm sorry. Why didn't you yell to me? You must have known I was here."

Only the silence of the kitchen answered back.

⁂

"Oh, Ruth! Fresh coffee! I think I must have died and gone to heaven," Dorie exclaimed the next morning as she sipped the steaming coffee while both women luxuriated in the smell and taste of it.

They were sitting at the table dawdling over a piece of sourdough bread, one piece each, without the butter or jam that had been their fare weeks before.

"Isn't it wonderful?" Ruth asked, smiling across at Dorie. As usual, Dorie's hair was a bit mussed and her plain face was thinner than before, but Ruth knew that her own face was thinner, as well. "I'm so grateful you are living with me, Dorie," she said, smiling at her friend.

"I'm the grateful one. Perish the thought of trying to survive in a boardinghouse filled with men. Isn't it amazing how everyone is opening their tiny cabins to take in a boarder in order to make an extra dollar?"

Ruth nodded. Her father had provided well for her, and for the first time she could truly appreciate what she had taken for granted most of her life.

"Speaking of boarders, have you met Jack London?" Dorie asked, her eyes bright.

Ruth thought back to the man who had come to her door with a note from Joe. "As a matter of fact, I have. Do you know him?"

"He dropped in at the newspaper office yesterday. He's a writer, you know. He left us a very good article he had written about life here in the territory. He's quite talented."

"Is he staying in town now?" she asked, thinking of Joe.

"Yes. As a matter of fact, I'll be seeing him again today or tomorrow. We'll have a small payment for him for his article."

"Dorie, would you ask him about Joe? His cabin is not far from Joe and Ivan's place."

"I'll be glad to," Dorie said, smiling at Ruth. "You've missed him, haven't you?"

Ruth nodded, averting her eyes. She was still haunted by the words Arthur had spoken. The Greenwoods were gossips. No doubt Mrs. Greenwood was confused about when the nuggets had been brought in to be assayed. Taking a deep breath, she looked back at Dorie. "I'm anxious to hear from him, but with the weather conditions, I don't expect that to happen anytime soon."

Dorie nodded, falling silent. Suddenly it occurred to Ruth what Dorie must be thinking. If so many other miners managed to get to Dawson, why couldn't Joe?

"Well, I must get busy," Dorie said, getting up from the table. "I'm spending the morning in my room. With the wind so brutal, I thought I would go through my box of clippings from Skagway. I never did do that article on survival. On Christmas Day, when I took the clippings over to the Fairhopes for my visit with them, we got sidetracked discussing London—they were there last year, you know. I confessed that I long to go some day, and the first thing I knew we were into a lengthy discussion of Europe. Well, in any case, this is the best time to write my article on survival. It was brutal in Skagway last winter. Many people died, but the important thing to remember is how many survived. That's what I want to cover in my article."

Ruth nodded. "Good idea. I'll try not to drop a dish to break your concentration."

They laughed and Dorie hurried out. Ruth smiled after her, thinking how she always moved at a rush. If ever there was a reason to be in no hurry now, the lifestyle in Dawson provided one.

An hour later, Ruth was kneading a fresh batch of sourdough when Dorie appeared in the kitchen door, an expression of horror on her face.

"Dorie, what is it?" Ruth asked, immediately sensing that something was terribly wrong.

For a moment, Dorie said nothing. She merely stared at Ruth. Then she looked down at the box of clippings she was holding, and Ruth realized that her stricken look was somehow connected to something she had read.

Reaching for a cup towel, Ruth wiped her hands and poured two cups of tea. "I can see that whatever is troubling you will require some tea and conversation."

Dorie walked slowly to the kitchen table and sat down, carefully placing the box on the table. As Ruth joined her, she glanced over the neatly clipped articles, wondering what Dorie had seen in those clippings that had upset her so badly.

"Ruth, I don't know how to tell you this," Dorie said, looking distressed.

"Tell me what?"

Dorie reached into the small pile of clippings and extracted one. Carefully, she laid it and a "Wanted" poster on the table, and what Ruth saw brought a gasp to her throat. She was looking into Joe's face. While he was heavily bearded, there was no mistaking the eyes or the hair or anything else about him. Except the name. Joe Whitworth.

"I. . .felt that I had seen him before when we met on Christmas Day," Dorie said slowly, her tone of voice heavy with regret. "What I didn't realize was that I had not actually seen him, only this. . . ."

Ruth was staring at the article, her heart beating wildly, her fingers trembling on the handle of the cup. It read:

*Joe Whitworth was arrested this morning and charged with the shooting of Austin Hankins after an argument erupted in the Dollarhide Saloon. . . .*

The tears that glazed Ruth's eyes made the print swim before her, so she stopped reading and looked at the picture of the other man, Austin Hankins. He had the kind of face one would not forget, an ugly face with long, hooked nose and narrow-set, angry eyes. She put a hand to her forehead, unable to read more, think more, feel more. One thought, however, was uppermost in her mind; and in the coming weeks, it never left her. It was something her father had said shortly before his death.

"Ruth, we don't really know Joe Spencer. . . ."

# eleven

Ruth had not touched the food Arthur had brought or the soup
Dorie had prepared the evening before, when Ruth had been
unable to cook. Sick at heart, Ruth had gone to bed, trying to
sort through her muddled thoughts. She so wanted to defend
Joe because she had loved him, but now she had to face the
fact that her father had spoken the truth: She did not know
him, not really. And if she did not know the real man, how
could she love the man he pretended to be? She couldn't, she
told herself. Yet, that did nothing to erase the terrible ache
that filled her heart.

If he was innocent of the crime, why had he escaped
Skagway, as the article went on to detail? And if there was
some mistake, why had he not confided the story to her?
Apparently Hankins had been a "colorful" local with dubious
connections, but still. . .

Another thought had taken root sometime during her sleep-
less night. She had given him the mining claim in good faith,
and she couldn't push aside the memory of Arthur's report:
that Joe had been into town with some promising nuggets
from one of his claims. Plural. What if that rich nugget was
from her claim? If so, it would explain why he had not come
to see her while he was in town. If he was a thief and a mur-
derer, he would not hesitate to take advantage of her. This
brought on more bitter tears.

Dorie had come home to see about her at noon. Ruth sat on
the sofa in the living room, staring into space, trying to put
herself back together. The sight of Dorie's face, however, did

nothing to cheer her. She looked even more downhearted than when she left this morning, offering a few cheerful words for Ruth in parting.

"Oh, Ruth," Dorie sighed as she entered the living room and took a seat opposite her. "I'm afraid I have more bad news."

"More?" Ruth echoed, wondering what could possibly be worse than what she had already heard. Her heart had been broken in half. Could she even feel anything now? Then she looked at her friend and her eyes widened as another fear took root. "Is something wrong with you, Dorie?" she asked suddenly.

"No, it isn't me," Dorie answered quickly. "Other than feeling a deep sadness for you, I am okay. It's just that. . .well, Jack London came into the newspaper office to pick up the payment for his article, and I asked him about Joe Spencer or Whitworth. . .or whoever he is. I remembered you mentioned he had a cabin nearby."

Ruth was torn with conflict. She wanted to hear about him and yet she could tell from Dorie's face that whatever she was about to tell her would only make matters worse.

"Go on," she said dully.

"Mr. London said Joe and his partner packed up and moved on. He didn't seem to know where or why."

"Where would they go?" Ruth asked incredulously. "I thought we were locked into the territory. No one can travel over the Pass now; there are no boats coming or going. . . ." Ruth's logic bogged down in the face of this latest news.

"Well," Dorie sighed, "it seems that a few miners—idiots it would appear—have taken another route out. Mr. London didn't seem to know much about it. All he knew was that the men were gone."

Ruth studied her hands, folded tightly in her lap. "I guess maybe he had reason to go," she said, taking a deep breath.

"Dorie, there's no point in trying to pretend it doesn't hurt, but I can see that I was completely taken in by this man. I always prided myself in being a good judge of character, but what is the saying? Pride goes before a fall."

Dorie reached out, gently touching Ruth's shoulder. "He was a charming man. I, too, was fooled by him. I wish there was something I could say or do to make matters better."

Ruth shook her head. "I'll get over it. But thanks for caring," she said, lifting her eyes to Dorie and hating the fact that she could no longer restrain the tears.

"There now," Dorie said comfortingly. "You'll get over it. I did," she said miserably as her eyes drifted thoughtfully. "I got my heart broken once, but in time one heals."

As tears poured down Ruth's cheeks, she looked at her friend and felt a fresh stab of pain. She hadn't known it was possible to feel this way about a man; now, she was learning what it was like to be hurt by that man. She swallowed hard, reaching into her pocket for a handkerchief. "You're right about one thing, Dorie. I will get over this."

But as the days dragged into weeks, Ruth began to wonder. It no longer mattered to her that there was little food in their pantry, for her appetite had vanished. She found that she was forcing herself to read the Bible, and she realized late one evening that she was mad at God, as well.

*How could You let me hurt this way?* her heart cried out.

And strangely, an answer whispered through her thoughts. *My child, I love you. I will never leave you nor forsake you.*

Huddled into her blankets to offset the cold of the house, for even the wood supply was getting low, Ruth took comfort from those words. She began to feel better because in her heart she felt the deep assurance that she was not alone. God had promised never to leave her alone or put on her heart more than she could bear.

æ

The snow fell in large flakes around him, quickly covering him. He had picked the warmest day of the month to ride into Dawson, and yet that day was brutal. By the time he reached the outskirts of town, he was frozen to the bone. Though he had been careful to keep himself well insulated with clothing, he knew it would take hours to feel warm again. That didn't matter to him. All that mattered was that he was on his way to see Ruth. And he had something very important to tell her.

He rode straight to her house, his heart hammering in his chest. It had been almost three months since he had seen her. During that time, life had been difficult. He and Ivan had worked in the brutal cold, enduring illness, suffering numbness in every joint, and once he had almost frozen to death by staying too long in the cold. Ivan had found him, dozing off against a tree, seeking the warmth that had begun to steal over him. Ivan had saved his life that night, and it had taken two weeks to recover, suffering a bout of influenza that had almost cost him his life a second time. Now he had recovered, and ever since moving up the creek to an abandoned shack near Ruth's claim, his heart had been filled to the bursting point. The claim was rich; he had been certain of it when Ivan brought in some nuggets for assaying while Joe lay sick on his cot. The news had helped to heal him, and now that he was stronger, he couldn't wait to share this good news with Ruth.

The sight of her log home brought a surge of joy as he turned his horse in at the hitching rail. Slowly, he climbed down, feeling as though his body was made of wood. Looping the leather reins over the post, he walked stiffly up the steps, eager to see the woman he loved. He had knocked several times before the door opened. Instead of facing Ruth, however, he was looking into Dorie Farmer's shocked face.

"Hello," he began, trying to force a stiff smile onto his

frozen lips. "Is Ruth home?"

Dorie stared at him for a moment, saying nothing, and he wondered if she had forgotten who he was. "I'm Joe Spencer and we met—"

"I remember our meeting," she answered coldly, "and I don't think Ruth will want to see you, but I will ask."

Her words stunned him, and he leaned against the door jamb when the door was suddenly closed in his face. What was wrong with this woman? Had she taken leave of her senses? Did she have him confused with someone else?

If he hadn't heard the key turn in the lock, he would have rudely thrust the door open and walked inside, calling out for Ruth. His mind was a fog of confusion as he waited anxiously for Ruth to come to the door. *Surely there must be some mistake. Surely—*

He heard the key turn in the lock and he straightened, eager to face the woman he loved. Again, it was Dorie Farmer who glared at him, and this time she shoved a newspaper clipping in his face. A quick glance told him more than he wanted to know. His heart sank. Slowly, his eyes moved back to Dorie's face, now contorted with anger.

"How dare you take advantage of a sweet, wonderful woman like Ruth. You've hurt her terribly. Don't ever come back to this house!" She slammed the door in his face, and this time he did not linger as the key turned in the lock.

There was nothing he could say or do, or if there was, he was too stunned to react. The moment he had feared and dreaded had finally come. The truth was out. And if Ruth and Dorie knew, it was only a matter of time until everyone in Dawson knew.

He felt as though he had aged ten years in a matter of minutes as he pulled himself wearily into the saddle and turned his horse toward the tiny log hut that served as the Dawson jail. He was tired of running, tired of hiding and pretending, tired of living. He had lost Ruth, and now nothing else mattered to him.

❧

Within the hour, Dawson was buzzing with the news: A notorious criminal had turned himself in; he would be returned to the authorities in Skagway as soon as weather permitted travel. The news was met with a mixture of feelings. The Greenwoods were smug with their conviction that the stranger had always acted a bit suspicious. Arthur Bradley was sorry for Ruth but dared hope she would take him seriously now. Miss Mattie and some of the men at the boardinghouse were shocked and saddened by the news, for those who had come to know him liked him.

It was Ruth who was troubled most by his surrender. She wondered why he had not kept on running, why he had bothered to surrender at this time. He had money, freedom, a chance at a new life. What had made him turn and do the right thing? Did she have anything to do with it? Did God? At one point, she would have swallowed her pride and gone to the jail to see him, if not for Dorie. Dorie was on a self-appointed mission to take care of Ruth until the boat pulled in, at which time Ruth was leaving Dawson. She had guarded the door, admitting only those Ruth wanted to see; she had even taken over some of the cooking, since Ruth had no interest in food. Most of all, she had warned Ruth that she would only make matters worse by showing up at the jail. There was nothing she could do for Joe Whitworth; and speaking from personal experience, she promised Ruth that the quicker she got over him, the better she would feel. Seeing him again would only open up the wound in her heart.

Listlessly, she packed up her possessions, eager to be ready when the Yukon thawed and the first boat came to Dawson.

Arthur Bradley frequently came to call, and she was glad to see him. If only she had not met Joe, she might have taken Arthur more seriously, she told herself. Perhaps she would have even fallen in love with him; then she would be accompanying him to lovely Victoria rather than going back to Seattle alone. Arthur had even broached the subject, but she had told him again, as gently as possible, that she felt only friendship. She knew this was true and that she could not have loved him, even if she had never met Joe.

&

As Joe sat in the jail cell day after day, feeling only misery and torment, he dared hope that Ruth would visit him. His only wish now was to tell her the truth, to try and explain things to her. He would take what was coming to him; he was willing to do that. He just couldn't bear for Ruth not to know his side of the story. In the long, dark hours of night, as he lay on the hard cot with the cold seeping through cracks in the walls, his soul ached even more than his body. He had gone to church with Ruth and felt again the stirring of God's love and the need to renew his spiritual life. He had even fought tears during the invitational hymn, but he had hardened his heart and ridden out of town. Now there was no place left to ride, no way out.

*God, if You'll have me, I want to come back to You,* he silently prayed. *Please forgive me for what I've done, and please help me to make amends to everyone I've hurt.*

Tears slipped down his thin, bearded cheeks, and soon his body shook with restrained sobs. The years of hurt that had built in his heart seemed to wash away with his tears, with the gentle cleansing power of God's healing love. The jail cell no longer seemed so lonely or so cold, and for the first time since his mother died, he felt a sense of peace take root in his heart.

&

Ruth stood at the wharf, waiting to board the *Bella* as it

slowly nudged its way into the dock. Shouts erupted throughout the crowd around her as the gangplank was lowered. At long last, the famine was over. Food, supplies, mail from home, and dozens of other delights awaited those in Dawson. For at least forty other people, eagerly gripping their tickets, the boat represented an escape out of the territory that had imprisoned them for the winter.

"Looks as though we'll have a bit of a wait," Arthur said, standing close beside Ruth. They were traveling together as far as Skagway, where they would each change boats again and head in opposite directions.

"Yes," Ruth agreed, recalling how Arthur had told her she had until Skagway to change her mind and go to Victoria to marry him. Feeling a sense of loneliness overtake her, she was tempted to accept his proposal. With mixed emotions, she turned and cast one last glance over the town where hammers pounded lumber once again, as tents were replaced by more log cabins. Briefly her eyes lingered on the tiny hut that served as the jail, and she thought of Joe.

A lump filled her throat. She still couldn't understand the pull she felt toward him, knowing what he had done. Dorie was right; it would take time to heal. She and Dorie had said tearful good-byes, for Dorie was remaining another week to complete a story on the reopening of Dawson. She would live in Ruth's house until then, at which time the missionaries coming to open the hospital would stay there. She had decided to donate the house to them for as long as they could use it. God had led her in this direction, and she had felt a sense of peace as soon as she made the decision.

Her eyes moved on to the cemetery on the hill, and the lump in her throat grew. She hated leaving her father here, but of course his soul had gone on to heaven, so she wasn't leaving him. She would join him some day.

Drawing a deep shaky breath, she turned her attention toward the arriving passengers, and suddenly one in particular caught her attention as he moved through the crowd. Directly in her line of vision, she studied him intently and then her breath caught. *It was him!*

She began to move toward him, scarcely aware of what she was doing, gawking at him like one who has never seen another human being. She was only vaguely aware of Arthur calling to her as she approached the thin, ugly man with long hair and beard, sharp hook nose, and narrow-set eyes.

"Excuse me," she said, stepping directly into his path to stop him. "Aren't you Austin Hankins?"

The narrow-set eyes widened momentarily as he looked her over. Then slowly he nodded. "Am I supposed to know you?" he asked.

"You aren't dead!" she exclaimed.

He stared at her as though she had lost her senses, and now Arthur stood beside her, staring at the man. "Ruth, what is it?"

"This man," she glanced at Arthur, "was not killed in Skagway. Joe didn't kill him, but he's being held for murder."

"He's here?" Hankins took a step back from her.

"In jail," Arthur was proud to volunteer.

"For your murder," Ruth repeated. "For some reason, you were assumed dead."

Hankins nodded. "I had my reasons for disappearing."

"But Spencer. . .or Whitworth. . .whoever he is. . . ran out," Arthur said, explaining this to Ruth rather than to the man.

"Never had to pay for what he did to me. And he should of paid!"

"He is paying now," Ruth said. "He has surrendered."

Hankins was the one to gawk now. "Why'd he do that? Surrender, I mean."

"Maybe he wanted to do the right thing. Don't you think it's time you did?"

Hankins snorted. "I ain't gettin' involved."

"You're already involved," she said, glaring at him.

He glanced toward the boat, as though considering heading back up the gangplank.

She spotted Lucky and a friend milling through the crowd, studying the boat and its passengers. He had turned in her direction and she waved to him.

"What is it, Miss Wright?" he asked, quickly approaching.

"This man," she indicated Hankins. "He's the one Joe is supposed to have killed. But as you can see, he's very much alive."

Hankins shifted from one foot to the other, his discomfort apparent as Lucky and his burly friend closed in on either side of him.

"Reckon we better mosey on down to the jail," Lucky said, taking his arm.

"Whitworth owes me for medical bills," he complained.

"Ruth, that is a matter between this man and the authorities." Arthur was tugging at her sleeve. "Come on, we can board the ship now."

Ruth yanked her arm free. "You go right ahead, Arthur. I'm going with these men to the jail. I think Mr. Hankins will want to give Joe Whitworth an opportunity to take care of his. . . *medical bills*."

"Ruth—"

"Arthur, please mind your own business," Ruth snapped, glaring at him.

This time he backed away from her, drew himself into a rigid stance, and looked at her with contempt. "I am through trying to reason with you. Good-bye, Ruth." He turned and stomped off, but Ruth didn't care. She was oblivious to everything except the man beside her. He was the type of man she would have avoided under other circumstances, but today he was the most special person in Dawson.

"Let's go." Lucky tugged the man's arm.

Sergeant Underwood bolted from his desk when they entered with Hankins in tow. His eyes widened as he looked at Hankins, as recognition flashed in his eyes.

Ruth was about to make the explanation when Hankins suddenly found his courage, which had been prompted, no doubt, by the fact that he wanted to exonerate himself of any charges.

"I hear you got a prisoner here, sir. There was a, er. . .a little misunderstanding in Skagway. I'm willing to drop charges against him under certain conditions."

The door was ajar that led to the cells, and Ruth's eyes locked on Joe's haggard face. He looked stunned for a moment, unable to believe what was happening. To her surprise, the anger she had felt for him began to fade. She was not ready to dismiss what he had done, but she felt a sense of relief in bringing the two men together.

The sound of the boat whistle jolted her back to her senses, and she turned to go.

"Ruth. . .wait," Joe called out.

She hesitated, her hand on her skirt. Slowly, she turned and looked at him again.

"Please give me a chance to explain. You owe me that." His eyes pleaded with her, and she felt powerless to walk out now, even though the boat's whistle sounded again, a warning for departing passengers to get on board.

Sergeant Underwood and Hankins were walking toward the cell, blocking Ruth's vision. "Is this the man?" he asked Hankins.

"Yep, he's the one."

"They said you were dead!" Joe said, gaping at him.

"And you were gonna swing from a rope," Hankins snorted.

Ruth could not stay out of it for another second, even though she tried. One question burned through her brain, and she had to know the answer. Then she would rush out, board the boat, and leave Dawson.

"Joe, why did you run?" Ruth asked, approaching the cell.

He looked into her eyes and shook his head. "I was weak and scared. I had been beating all those men in poker for over a week. They hated me. I knew everyone would back up his story. Hankins pulled a gun first," he said, turning to Sergeant Underwood. "I fired back in self-defense, but no one would believe that, either. Then he disappeared, and one of his buddies said he died as a result of the gunshot after he was taken back to camp. They said they buried him there," he added bitterly, "and everyone believed them. Even I believed them," he added on a heavy sigh. "Then when the deputy fell asleep with my cell unlocked, I couldn't help myself."

"Whitworth, this fella is willing to drop charges against you." Underwood took over again. "The provision is that you pay for his medical expenses."

"Medical expenses?" Joe asked bitterly.

"Yep. I had some big medical expenses," Hankins crowed.

"I'm going to wire the authorities in Skagway," Underwood stated. "They may still request a trial."

"Why?" Hankins looked disappointed. "I'm alive. I ain't pressing charges if he pays for my medical expenses."

"I'll do that," Joe said, looking at Ruth.

The sound of the boat whistle was more vague now, and Ruth heard it with less concern. It wouldn't hurt to wait another week and leave with Dorie, she decided. Then she remembered her trunk, abandoned at the dock.

"I must go," she said.

"Ruth!" Joe was staring at her cranberry woolen dress and matching hat. "Are you leaving Dawson?"

She took a deep breath. "Not today. I'll wait a week to see what is going to happen to you."

She started to say more but restrained herself. She would give him a week; somehow, she felt she owed him that. She had been taught by her parents to always be fair, and as a Christian, she tried to be a forgiving person. In good faith, she felt she had to give him one last chance. One more week in Dawson would not change her life, whereas if she left now, never to see him again, she knew her life would drastically change. For in that ten minutes that she had stood in the jail, looking into his pleading eyes, she knew she still cared for him.

&

On Sunday, after the church service, Ruth and Joe sat in the living room of her house. Dorie had tactfully disappeared to her room to work on her newspaper article. So much had happened in the past few days that Ruth's head was still spinning. Still, she forced herself to listen to Joe as he spoke calmly and looked at her with eyes that begged forgiveness.

"I know it will take a while to regain your trust, but I'm coming to you now as a different man. God finally got my attention," he said, with a wry grin.

"And you rededicated your life this morning at church," she said, smiling at him. "Even the pastor thinks I should forgive you, so what choice do I have?"

"Don't tease me, Ruth," he said earnestly.

She took his hand. "I'm sorry. You've been through enough. I think it's time to put the past behind us and get on with our lives."

"Now that I've made my settlement with Hankins, I'd like permission from you to continue working your claim this summer, Ruth. It's a rich one, and by the time the boat leaves at the end of the summer, we could have a real nest egg for that ranch." He dropped his head. "I'm sorry. I'm assuming too much. It's your money."

"Excuse me, but I believe we had a deal."

He looked up, startled.

"We're partners, remember? Half of the proceeds of that claim belong to you. You could have your own nest egg."

He took her hand in his and moved closer. "Ruth, I've dreamed of a ranch for years. How do you feel about that?"

She smiled. "I could feel good about that. . .if I were with the man I love."

Joe took her into his arms, tilting her chin back and smiling into her face. "I don't know what I ever did to deserve a person like you, but I promise you, as God is our witness, I will be the best Christian I can possibly be. And the best husband," he added.

Tears filled her eyes. "Joe, I've always prayed to have the kind of relationship my parents had. I know God blessed their marriage because their lives were dedicated to pleasing Him. I do love you, and now that you have come back to God, I feel we have a chance for real happiness." She put her hand to his cheek, gently stroking his clean-shaven face. "Must I wait until the end of the summer to put you to the test? About being a good husband?"

He laughed. "Of course not. Nothing would make me happier than to get married right away. If you're planning to stay on here and help get the missionary hospital going, then I can be a weekend guest, if that's okay with you."

"That's fine with me," she said, smiling into his eyes as he lowered his lips to kiss her.

❧

Peering through a crack in the door, Dorie felt like a mischievous child, and yet seeing the two together again, happy and so in love, warmed her heart. And it gave her new hope. Ruth and Joe had been given a second chance at happiness.

Dorie smiled, quietly closing the door. Maybe someday it would happen to her.

# A Letter To Our Readers

Dear Reader:

In order that we might better contribute to your reading enjoyment, we would appreciate your taking a few minutes to respond to the following questions. We welcome your comments and read each form and letter we receive. When completed, please return to the following:

Rebecca Germany, Fiction Editor
Heartsong Presents
PO Box 719
Uhrichsville, Ohio 44683

1. Did you enjoy reading *Silent Stranger?*
   ☐ Very much. I would like to see more books
   by this author!
   ☐ Moderately
   I would have enjoyed it more if _____
   _____
   _____

2. Are you a member of **Heartsong Presents**? Yes ☐ No☐
   If no, where did you purchase this book?_____
   _____

3. How would you rate, on a scale from 1 (poor) to 5 (superior), the cover design?_____

4. On a scale from 1 (poor) to 10 (superior), please rate the following elements.

   _____ Heroine        _____ Plot

   _____ Hero           _____ Inspirational theme

   _____ Setting        _____ Secondary characters

5. These characters were special because _____

_____

_____

6. How has this book inspired your life? _____

_____

_____

7. What settings would you like to see covered in future
   **Heartsong Presents** books? _____

_____

_____

8. What are some inspirational themes you would like to see
   treated in future books? _____

_____

_____

9. Would you be interested in reading other **Heartsong
   Presents** titles?          Yes ❏              No ❏

10. Please check your age range:
    ❏ Under 18          ❏ 18-24              ❏ 25-34
    ❏ 35-45             ❏ 46-55              ❏ Over 55

11. How many hours per week do you read? _____

Name _____

Occupation _____

Address _____

City _____ State _____ Zip _____

*What they find on America's vast plains is not what they expected—but it's more than they ever dared to dream.*

The wide-open plains of the Dakota Territory form the setting for the lives and loves of four inspiring women making their way in the New World. This captivating volume combines three of bestselling author Lauraine Snelling's novels under one cover, along with a bonus novella.

Journey with these courageous women as they make their homes in the Dakota plains—and allow God to fulfill the desires of their hearts in unexpected ways.

400 pages, Paperbound, 5 ³⁄₁₆" x 8"

# ·········· Presents ··········

## Great Inspirational Romance at a Great Price!

**Heartsong Presents** books are inspirational romances in contemporary and historical settings, designed to give you an enjoyable, spirit-lifting reading experience. You can choose wonderfully written titles from some of today's best authors like Peggy Darty, Sally Laity, Tracie Peterson, Colleen L. Reece, Lauraine Snelling, and many others.

*When ordering quantities less than twelve, above titles are $2.95 each.*
*Not all titles may be available at time of order.*

# Heartsong Presents
## Love Stories Are Rated G!

That's for godly, gratifying, and of course, great! If you love a thrilling love story, but don't appreciate the sordidness of some popular paperback romances, **Heartsong Presents** is for you. In fact, **Heartsong Presents** is the *only inspirational romance book club*, the only one featuring love stories where Christian faith is the primary ingredient in a marriage relationship.

Sign up today to receive your first set of four, never before published Christian romances. Send no money now; you will receive a bill with the first shipment. You may cancel at any time without obligation, and if you aren't completely satisfied with any selection, you may return the books for an immediate refund!

Imagine. . .four new romances every four weeks—two historical, two contemporary—with men and women like you who long to meet the one God has chosen as the love of their lives. . .all for the low price of $9.97 postpaid.

*To join, simply complete the coupon below and mail to the address provided.* **Heartsong Presents** romances are rated G for another reason: They'll arrive *Godspeed!*